The Lake of Fire

Other books of
The Mogi Franklin Mysteries
Ghosts of the San Juan
The Lost Children
The Secret of La Rosa
The Hidden River

The Lake of Fire

Donald Willerton

Terra Nova Books
SANTA FE, NEW MEXICO

Library of Congress Control Number 2017945951

Distributed by SCB Distributors, (800) 729-6423

Terra Nova Books

Published by Terra Nova Books, Santa Fe, New Mexico.
www.TerraNovaBooks.com

ISBN 978-1-938288-89-0

For My Mother

CHAPTER

Denver, Colorado
August 24, 1963

A small plane was pulled into a hangar at a private airport north of Denver. The tall doors rolled shut, and two heavily-armed men took their positions outside.

A half-dozen technicians began loading the plane with metal cases that had been delivered an hour earlier from the Rocky Flats Plant, Denver's nuclear fuels manufacturing facility only a few miles away. The cases, each about the size of a suitcase, needed to be more than three hundred miles south, in Los Alamos, New Mexico, by daybreak.

The eight-passenger, twin-engine Beechcraft had five seats removed to accommodate the load. Each case, specifically designed for transporting nuclear materials, was marked with the glaring black-and-yellow markings "DANGER!" and "RADIATION —HANDLE WITH CARE!" Inside each case, thin sheets of nuclear material were layered with lead shielding. Surrounded by an airtight barrier and packed securely, each case weighed more than a hundred pounds.

In total, the cases held two hundred pounds of highly refined plutonium, enough to keep the researchers and bomb designers at Los Alamos busy in the fierce, day-to-day battles of the Cold War.

The Soviets had just exploded a 58-megaton bomb, almost 3000 times more powerful than the Hiroshima and Nagasaki bombs and more powerful than any weapon in the United States' nuclear arsenal. A small tidal wave of panic swept through the White House and the Pentagon, and now everybody was hopping. The pressure for bigger bombs and more of them had increased like steam in a kettle. If the United States were to keep its lines of defense strong, if it were to maintain that precious perception of nuclear superiority, it needed more missiles, more warheads, and bigger booms.

And they needed it yesterday.

The pilot and co-pilot of the Beechcraft worked the checklist. Major Henry Samples, an Air Force flight commander, was the pilot. He had flown everything with wings, and there wasn't a better man to fly the backcountry skies of Colorado and New Mexico.

Christopher Johnson was the co-pilot, an experienced ex-military flyboy with the added advantage of being a materials expert at the lab in Los Alamos. It was routine for him to go along with secret shipments of nuclear materials around the United States or over to the atomic test islands in the Pacific. He was confident and casual. Settling in his seat, he was already relaxing for what he expected would be a short, easy flight.

The third man in the plane was a typical government babysitter. He'd be CIA or FBI or some other three-letter branch of the government and would sit silently in his seat, always with a nervous look and a suspicious eye.

Chris Johnson watched a second plane on the other side of the hangar. Identical to the one he was in, showing the same aircraft identification markings on the outside, it was being loaded with a set of six identical yellow cases with identical markings, exactly matched to the cases being loaded into his plane. One set of the cases held the plutonium; the other set held sheets of useless lead.

The pilots and co-pilots didn't know which cases were which, and they assumed the babysitters didn't know either. Only the guys in the big offices at Rocky Flats knew which plane carried the real stuff. As might be expected, the three men inside the second plane wore uniforms identical to Henry, Chris, and the other man. The smallest detail was identical. At least, those were the rules.

But Chris Johnson always managed to have one small difference—a flyer's insignia pinned on his jacket. He never flew without it, pinning it on when no one was looking. It was the traditional flyer's pin, two silver wings surrounding a red "A" for aviator. He had received the pin upon graduation from flight school. Becoming a pilot had meant a lot to him and to his wife, Mary. Going to flight school wasn't easy when you were married, and it took both of them to get him through.

He wore the pin for her.

During the taxiing out to the runway, the crews of the planes went over the switching procedures. They would fly together, one in front of the other, and at least once during the flight, the planes would switch positions. It was unplanned and could happen at any time. Either of the government agents— the "third man"—could issue a command to exchange positions, and the pilots would obey. Dreamed up by some security guy in Washington, it gave an air of devilish trickery to the operation and added to the illusion of absolute security for any congressman to whom it was explained.

The pilots thought it was nonsense.

The two planes motored onto the runway, lined up, pushed their engines to the max, and lifted off in perfect cadence. As soon as they left the airport airspace, the babysitter spoke and Henry slipped in behind the now-designated lead plane. The ground crew listened as the drone of the planes faded into the quiet of the night sky.

The flight plan was simple: out to the southwest, above Highway 285, slide over the peaks of the Mosquito Range, go dead south through the Arkansas River basin, over the bump of Poncha Pass, past Alamosa on the left, down the Rio Grande valley, and into the Los Alamos airport.

Chris looked at the clock on the instrument panel and quickly calculated the time schedule for the rest of the night. A couple of hours to the Los Alamos airport; a few minutes to unload; the inspection of the cases, along with the umpteen pieces of paper that had to be completed and signed; and the required debriefing session with the transport chief. After that, the lab's storage people would take over and he'd be out of there.

It would be mid-morning when he got home. A little nap and he'd be ready for a weekend in Albuquerque. With the latest pressures from the bureaucrats, he had been riding transport planes too often for Mary's liking. She was tired of his being gone. With a baby on the way, it was even worse. Maybe he could make it up to her this weekend. In fact, he didn't have anything significant on Monday; maybe it was time for a little R&R in the big town.

It was a superb night to fly. The upper air currents were calm; the lights below were few and the sky clear. No winds buffeted them as they slid over the mountaintops and into the river valley. A steady tailwind had them ten minutes ahead of schedule when Poncha Pass silently slipped by below them.

Chris looked out on the ocean of stars. Without a moon, he couldn't quite make out where the dark of the land became the dark of the sky. The plane in front flew with normal lights; the second plane, behind by 500 yards, flew with lights off, appearing only as a dark patch of nothing against the stars of the night sky.

Henry watched the quiet town of Alamosa in the distance, and then gingerly maneuvered around the big bump known as San Antonio Mountain. They were in New Mexico and just about home.

As the two planes steadily droned over the New Mexico-Colorado border, the government man in the back—"Bill" as he had given his name—unzipped his flight jacket, reached under his armpit and removed his pistol. Inserted into a hidden sleeve inside the holster was a smaller device, a transmitter that he now quietly slid into his palm.

"Time to switch," he said quietly, leaning forward.

Henry Samples picked the radio handset off the console, pressed the button, and spoke a few words. Increasing his speed as he pulled back on the control, he moved the plane directly above the plane in front of him, ready for the other plane to decrease speed and settle in behind.

As Henry moved directly over the first plane, the government babysitter, who was no babysitter at all, pressed a small button on the transmitter. If anyone on the ground below had been listening, the noise of the two planes would have suddenly grown much quieter.

Quieter by half.

Only one plane continued. The engines of the lower plane suddenly quit and the controls were rendered useless. The lower plane slammed into the valley floor below.

Henry was puzzled by the lack of a voice in his earphones. He tried several calls to the other plane before he felt the cold barrel of a pistol pressed into his neck. "Bill," who had inched up to the space between the seats, gave simple instructions.

"Go into a steep dive, level at eight thousand feet, and turn west. Now. Leave the lights off."

It was a convincing threat, and Henry did as he was told. Chris sat in bewildered stillness as the gun barrel moved across the space and now rested behind his own neck.

Eight thousand feet. In a country of ten- and eleven-thousand-foot mountains, that meant flying just above tree height through the dark canyons that twisted like the run of a bobsled.

Two hundred miles south, the radar at the big airport in Albuquerque had picked up the two planes as they came over San Antonio Mountain and into the broad expanse of the Rio Grande valley. As the sweep hand on the radar console rotated slowly around, two little blips moved down the green screen. The radar operator had been told to watch for the blips but not to communicate or call for their identity. The Los Alamos airport would let him know if they needed him.

So, it was only with casual interest that he watched the two blips become one. He was a little more interested when the blip blinked a bright green spot one moment and didn't appear at all the next. He was wondering if he should tell somebody when, out his window, the hangars of Kirtland Air Force Base next door lit up like a Christmas tree, and a screeching wail of a scramble siren shattered the quiet of the night. Before he understood what was going on, two fighter jets roared down the runway with an emergency clearance.

It was only a minute or two from the disappearance of the last blip on the screen to the time the fighter jets shot into the air. It took seven minutes more for them to cover the hundred and sixty miles to the location of the last blip.

But it was still enough time for one plane, three men, and two hundred pounds of the most dangerous metal on earth to vanish into thin air.

CHAPTER
2

Los Alamos, New Mexico
Present Day

So that's what the famous atomic bomb looked like—a giant football with fins.

There were two atomic bombs dropped on Japan to end World War II. The big one, called Fat Man—identical in appearance to the empty casing Mogi Franklin was standing next to—had been dropped on the city of Nagasaki. The other bomb, called Little Boy, was about a third the size of its big brother, and its empty casing was behind him. It had been dropped on the city of Hiroshima a few days before. Between the two, they represented the only nuclear weapons in the history of mankind to be used in war.

Mogi's fingertips tingled at the cold of the painted metal as he ran his hands up and down and around the smooth, glossy surface, standing on his tip-toes to touch the top, leaning over and still not touching the bottom.

He stood back and took a couple of pictures with his phone.

He was glad he and Jennifer had signed up for the program. The National High School Institute for the Environmental Sciences was being held at the Valles Caldera Conference Center in New Mexico, right in the middle of a hundred thousand acres of the Valles Caldera National Preserve and surrounded by a ring of eleven-thousand-foot mountains. Twenty-four students from middle schools and high schools in Utah and Arizona had been invited to the week-long, government-sponsored program to introduce them to careers related to the environment.

"You'd better hurry up, dweeb," Phil Agnew said as he walked by, slapping the back of Mogi's head.

Mogi whipped around as he watched the big kid walk off. At nineteen, Phil worked as a summer assistant at the institute and was a chaperone for the visit to the museum.

Mogi burned a little with the slap but let it go. If Phil was picking on him, then Phil was picking on everybody. It had taken Mogi less than a minute at the conference center to recognize that Phil was a jerk. He was bossy, insulting, and rough, and seemed offended that he had to lower himself to a job that involved working with "kids."

Classic jerk.

He and Jennifer had arrived that morning. Brother and sister, they were from Bluff, Utah, close to the Four Corners area where the borders of New Mexico, Arizona, Utah, and Colorado meet. It was bare rock country—hundreds of square miles of bare sandstone, with solitary mesas rising a thousand feet out of the desert floor and an uncountable number of craggy, twisting canyons.

Mogi was fourteen and tall for his age, but his muscles had not yet caught up with his bones, so he was gangly and spindly and a little bit awkward, which is to say, normal for his position in life. He took after his mom's side of the family in his looks and his shyness, but seemed to be a sum of both families on the brain side: he was way smarter than most of the people around him. Quick-minded, mentally disciplined, and orderly, he had a natural talent for solving puzzles.

After he and Jennifer had gotten settled into the dorms, attended the program's orientation, and had lunch at the conference center's dining hall, they and the others were shuttled to the science museum in Los Alamos, about twenty miles to the east, over a mountain pass.

The museum featured the history of the town and the Manhattan Project, the super-secret effort during World War II to design, build, and drop an atomic bomb. Nobody in the world knew what was going on until they dropped the first one in August of 1945.

More than seventy years after the town of Los Alamos was created to house the Manhattan Project and its scientists and their families, the original wooden shacks and the wooden water tower that was famous for freezing during the winter had been replaced with more than eight hundred modern buildings across forty-three square miles. The Los Alamos National Laboratory had become a world-class research organization dedicated not only to nuclear weapons development, but also environmental science, metallurgy, space, computers, computer modeling, chemistry, genetics, health, and many other research areas.

"Have you started your list? I've already got six things. Betcha that's more than you've got."

John Travers had come up behind him. John was from somewhere south of Flagstaff, Arizona. Not giving Mogi a chance to answer, the boy turned and walked quickly away. That was OK, since Mogi wasn't about to show him his blank notebook page. The students' first assignment was to make a list of ten items at the museum that were connected to an environmental issue.

Making a list wouldn't be a problem, Mogi thought. Lists are one thing that I'm good at. He kept looking at the war exhibit. The display around the bomb casings had copies of different newspapers from the World War II era. Armies all over the place, concentration camps, the shelling of London, the bombing raids on Berlin, the incredibly complex ship battles at sea in the Pacific, the horrific combat on various islands, the massive reaction of America to Pearl Harbor. It presented a picture of the utter gruesomeness of war.

Mogi passed under a mock-up of a cruise missile hanging from the ceiling and in front of another display. Large, white letters caught his eye: "Nuclear Weapons Accidents." There have been about thirty accidents involving U.S. nuclear weapons: several bomber crashes, a Minuteman missile blowing up in its silo in Arkansas, and one bomb whose holding mechanism snapped during a flight, causing the bomb to rip right through the bottom of the airplane. Several bombs have been accidentally or deliberately dropped at sea. None caused a nuclear explosion, and most of the accidents ended with the bombs being recovered. But not all. One time, a B-52 bomber from the Strategic Air Command had a major engine failure and was going to crash into the Pacific Ocean. The crew released a pair of bombs just before the airplane hit the water because it was "safer" than keeping them inside a crashing plane. The crew survived, but the bombs were never found

They're still there, Mogi thought—still at the bottom of the ocean.

"You'd better hurry." It was Jennifer. "We've only got twenty minutes before we have to be back on the bus." She knew that if she didn't keep reminding him, her brother would read every word of every poster. He wouldn't notice anything until they turned off the lights.

Jennifer was seventeen, three years older than Mogi, and definitely took after her father. Shorter than her brother by a half-foot, with thick, brown hair cut short, she was strong, athletic, physically graceful, had a keen sense of compassion, and loved being around people. If Mogi was the obsessive analytical, adventurous problem-solver, Jennifer was the cautious, emotionally-centered people-person. He pushed her to do more than she thought she ought to; she pulled him back to what was reasonable.

"OK, OK, I'll get to it." He really wanted to read more, but Jennifer had a point. Maybe he could come back before the week was up.

Mogi moved to the next display: "Nuclear Espionage: The Spies Within."

The sign was in bold red letters against a black background and hung above a wall covered with pictures and captions. A smaller sign introduced it as a new exhibit.

It featured stories about spies over the years. There were spies everywhere—every nation had theirs, the United States had ours—all the time. There were even spies working within the Manhattan Project itself, working right alongside the scientists and technicians in Los Alamos and other secret places across the United States. With the end of the Cold War and the break up of the Soviet Union in the '80s, many details were just being learned about the Soviet spy network in the states. Espionage was a game that every nation played. That was normal business between enemies, and sometimes even friends.

There was a gasp behind him.

"I can't believe they did that! This is absolutely wrong! They are not going to get away with this!"

A woman behind him had swung around on her heel, dropping a notebook on the floor as she did so. She headed toward the entry desk where a receptionist sat.

It was Dr. Simpson, the head of the Institute's summer program who had given the orientation talk before lunch. She supervised all the activities at the environmental science camp. She worked for the lab as an environmental scientist and managed several of the lab's other high-school programs. Overall, she seemed really nice, calm, easy-going, and smart.

She certainly wasn't calm now.

He watched her as she marched up to the receptionist and bombarded her with questions. "What do you mean putting up something like that? There is no proof! Where's the museum director? I want to see him right now."

Everyone was staring at her, trying to act as if they weren't. Dr. Simpson, or Nancy, as she wanted the students to call her, was ushered off behind a door marked Staff Only, and the crowd watched as the door swung closed. Mogi picked up her notebook. He would give it to her later.

What had made her so angry? He looked at the exhibit. Whatever it was, it had to be right in front of him—she had been reading the same display.

It was an enlargement of an old photograph, showing what seemed to be a warehouse with a group of men standing around a forklift. A circle was superimposed on a large, metal shelf behind the men. On the shelf were six yellow containers about the size of large suitcases. Only the one in front could be fully seen. It had a large radiation sign on the side.

The text under the photograph read:

Largest Theft of Plutonium in History

In August of 1963, United States Air Force Major Henry Samples and Los Alamos Laboratory materials scientist Christopher Johnson accomplished the daring theft of two hundred pounds of refined plu-

tonium, the largest hijacking of nuclear materials in American history. During a transfer of plutonium from the Rocky Flats manufacturing facility near Denver, Colorado, to Los Alamos, the two men diverted a cargo plane to a secret rendezvous with Russian conspirators high in the Jemez Mountains west of Los Alamos. Under the cover of night, they delivered the plutonium to Russian agents who then smuggled it to the Soviet Union. The two men escaped in the plane and were never seen again. In 1968, in a photo deliberately leaked to the United States government, the Russians revealed that they had, indeed, scored a clear victory of espionage over the American nuclear community. Samples and Johnson were convicted, in their absence, of high treason against the United States.

Two hundred pounds of plutonium. The Fat Man bomb across the room hadn't used anywhere close to that.

"Mogi!" his sister called, coming up behind him. "We've got to go. They're calling us to the bus. Come on."

Walking in the direction of the front door, Mogi weaved his way around other exhibits. He weaved right into Phil Agnew.

"Get a move on, dweeb, or we're going to leave you behind. I guess they let anybody over ten into these conferences. What am I going to have to do to make you understand how to follow orders, huh?"

Mogi turned away as quickly as he could and walked in a different direction. He looked at exhibit titles as he passed by. The Human Genome, Waste Handling (that was environmental), Medical Research, Nuclear Power from Lasers (that's probably one), Fluid Modeling, Electric Cars (that's another one), Oil Recovery, Air Monitoring and Wildlife Surveys and Radiation Exposure and Paper Recycling and In Ground Vitrification (what?).

Stepping onto the bus, Mogi sat in one of the front seats since the other seats behind were taken. Dr. Simpson came in last and slid into the seat beside him. She was still flushed with emotion.

"Uh, I have your notebook," he said, handing it to her.

"Oh, thank you," she said. "I'm afraid I was quite an embarrassment."

"Nah. I don't think anybody noticed," he lied. He really wanted to know more, but figured it wasn't any of his business. On the other hand, if he didn't ask, he'd never know.

"I was just wondering," he began in a halting voice, "what you thought of the display about the spies. I thought it was pretty interesting."

"Well, it's interesting if you're not concerned with the truth. I get so irritated with these people. Did you read the part about the stealing of the plutonium? By two men who disappeared with the plane?" she asked.

"Yeah. About two hundred pounds."

"Well, they didn't steal anything. Neither one of them could have ever done that. They were good and loyal men. These people have the story all wrong."

She stared out the window as the bus passed through the main part of town, over a bridge, and then headed toward the mountains.

"Just because they never found the plane doesn't mean that they defected to Russia. They know the photo in the warehouse is a fake and they still can't see past their noses to admit that maybe everything else is wrong, too. They won't even consider that the plutonium wasn't stolen."

Did she mean the photo had been doctored or staged? Why would Russia want us to think they had stolen the shipment if they hadn't?

"But I can't prove anything well enough to convince anybody," she said as she turned to him and then turned back to the window. "But I know it wasn't them."

She turned to him again. "Christopher Johnson, the scientist from the lab?"

Mogi nodded. Samples and Johnson.

"He was my father."

Nancy became silent and Mogi turned his attention to the bus as it swayed along the winding road. As they lifted out of the flat mesas, the highway grew steeper, narrower, and cut a contour across the sloping sides of the mountains. The forest became more dense. Mogi could see pine trees that were easily a hundred feet tall.

Crossing over the pass and coming down into the valley surrounded by the peaks, he looked across several miles of broad, knee-high grass. The preserve had some of the biggest elk herds in the United States, as well as an abundance of deer and bear and mountain lions.

Watching the scenery as it went by, he tried to recall more of the orientation talk, but his mind kept wandering back to the woman beside him.

The biggest theft of plutonium in history and I'm sitting next to the crook's daughter.

Why did she think everyone was wrong?

CHAPTER

I t was Sunday evening. Mogi made it through the dishes return line and was out the door to catch the group in front of him. He had jotted down a few titles from the exhibits at the science museum. His mom said that his memory was a gift. Talent or gift or just lucky, he could remember things like crazy. It was like his brain took a picture and, even if he hadn't been paying attention, he could call up that picture and look at it in his mind.

The group crossed from the dining hall to the general education building that held the lecture hall. The dorms were to the right, up a hill, and closer to the trees, while the education building was across the main road.

The preserve had once been a huge cattle ranch owned by some millionaire in Texas. Cattle were brought up in the spring to feed on the rich grasslands for the summer and then taken back to Texas for the winter. The original ranch headquarters building was about a quarter-mile from the education building and included a big barn surrounded by cattle pens and a large, two-storied log house beyond it. Several smaller buildings were clustered on the other side.

In 2000, the government bought the ranch and declared it the Valles Caldera National Preserve. Dedicating it to a wide range of uses, the preserve management built a modern, fully-equipped conference center to host federal educational programs, university and college research teams, national conferences, leadership and management retreats, and other activities.

In addition to operating the conference center and its facilities, the ranch continued as a working cattle ranch, keeping a regular crew of cowboys and a herd of about a thousand cows. The money from profits went back into the ranch operations.

After the group was gathered in the auditorium, Dr. Simpson—Nancy, as she reminded them—listed issues on a white board as she led a discussion with the students.

"What does the list tell us?" she asked.

"The lab does a lot of stuff."

"Everything's connected to the environment."

"Science is important."

"Get rid of nuclear weapons."

"Respect the environment; it's our legacy to our children."

"Go to school so you can make lots of money as a scientist."

The last response brought a laugh.

Talking about each item on the list, Nancy built a diagram to identify how much more knowledge was needed in almost every aspect of the environment. She told stories about her work at the laboratory, some of the research being done in other countries, and how the importance of protecting and preserving the environment needed to become part of everyone's thinking if we were to survive as a global community.

Mogi liked the talk, and he liked her. He listened as well as he could, but his mind kept going back to the incident at the museum. Where had she grown up? What did her mother do after her father disappeared? What really happened? Where did the plane go? Didn't it have to land somewhere and refuel?

Could it have flown all the way to Mexico? How did the Russians get the plutonium out of the country?

"You're not listening," his sister said as she poked him.

"I'm still thinking about the museum thing," he whispered. "I want to know more about what happened."

"That was a long time ago. What do you want to know for?" she whispered.

"You should have seen Dr. Simpson's face when she told me that one of the guys was her father. I mean, she looked a hundred years old, like she was so sorry that she couldn't prove him innocent, like she wanted it more than anything in the world."

"Uh-oh, you're getting curious, aren't you? Well, just remember that the greatest minds in the world have worked this problem for a lot of years, and what you saw is what they ended up with. Dr. Simpson may be wishing for more than history can give her, and you shouldn't be thinking that you need to help."

Nancy got everybody's attention.

"If each of you will reach under the edge of your seat, you will find a card taped to the bottom with a number on it. The number tells you what team you are on.

"I want everyone to stand and the people on Team One to move to that corner, those on Team Two to move to that corner," she went on, dividing up the students around the room. There were four teams of six students each, along with an adult staffer as the team leader and one teen-age staffer as helper.

Mogi pulled his card out and could hardly keep from jumping up and down. He had landed on the team with Nancy as the adult leader. His stomach then hit the floor—Phil Agnew was his team helper.

"Your team," Nancy continued, "is your working unit for the week. Each team has an adult and a staff assistant. These two will help your team through the week, but they will not be making team decisions for you. You'll work through your team assignments together, you'll go on trips together, you'll do activities together, you'll do your research together, and you'll do team chores together. You will learn to rely on each other. Each of you will develop a specific role within your team, and it will take the whole team to bring your week to a successful conclusion. You will become your own community."

The assistants passed out a packet of information for each team. It had several handouts and information sheets listing the various team objectives for the week, the activities, and the schedule.

The team members introduced each other.

"I'm Mogi Franklin, from Bluff, Utah. That's on the San Juan River close to Four Corners."

"My name is Sharon Thompson, and I'm from Green River, Utah."

"My name is Henry Begay, from Tuba City."

The introductions continued around the circle: John Mitchell, from Sedona; Charlotte Manygoats, from Kayenta; Ernie Grimes, from Kingman.

Four from Arizona, two from Utah, Nancy the leader, and Phil the jerk.

CHAPTER

By supper on Tuesday, Mogi wanted Nancy Simpson's job. Monday was River Day, spent hiking along the East Jemez River, a stream flowing through the preserve. The group spent the day gathering water samples; measuring flow rates and water temperatures; writing up insect finds; collecting fish with nets, counting, measuring and releasing them; describing the vegetation; and then mapping the stream as it entered a deep canyon.

Tuesday was Rock Day. It started with a presentation by a geologist who explained that the preserve was the interior of a huge volcano that had erupted and then collapsed. Viewing slides of different rock features throughout the area, the group discussed what the images revealed about the layers of rock beneath the ranch property. Afterward, the team was driven fifteen miles to an area where they spent two hours gathering fossils from various dry creek beds.

"And then we went to a bunch of hot springs where we sat and roasted in the water for a while," he told Jennifer at supper. "Then we went to see the Fenton Hill geothermal site, where they drill deep holes in the ground, bring up super-heated water, and drive turbines to generate electricity. It was great!"

"OK, OK," Jennifer said. "You don't know what great is. Just wait until tomorrow, when you have Muck."

Jennifer's team had done Rock Day on Monday and Ranch Day on Tuesday. On Thursday, the teams would combine to do Mountain Day, which featured an overnight hike into the mountains.

"What's muck?" Mogi asked.

"Not what, who. Muck's a name. Muck Jones. You're going to like him. He's the foreman of the ranch and is quite a character. He does the tour of the ranch operations and leads the horse-packing trip."

Nancy joined Mogi and Jennifer at their dining table. "Are you two interested in a little side trip tonight?" she asked.

"You bet!" Mogi replied before Jennifer had a chance to speak.

"Remember my problem with the museum?" Nancy continued. "They've asked me to meet with the exhibit committee to make a case for either removing that part of the exhibit or changing the wording. After all of the questions you've had this week," she said to Mogi, "I thought you'd like to hear the whole story."

Mogi smiled and nodded. There wasn't anything he wanted more. During the past two days, even though he tried not to, he couldn't help but ask her questions about the stolen plutonium.

Thirty minutes later, as the Suburban left the ranch and made its way along the twisting highway through the mountains, Nancy told stories of the early settlers of the area and then the years during the war. "You had some of the smartest people in the world, all working on something that had never been done before."

"What was it like growing up here?" Jennifer asked.

"Oh, I didn't grow up in Los Alamos. My Mom and I moved away after my Dad disappeared. I didn't come back till 1990 to start working at the lab."

As Nancy explained to Jennifer and Mogi how she chose her career, Mogi watched the trees and meadows, wondering how long the forest had been there, where all the animals lived, what winter was like. It was peaceful and serene, a world to itself.

"The forest looks dry," he said.

"That's for sure," Nancy said. "The whole state is in a long-term drought. We haven't had a good snow season for the past few years, and our rainfall has been only a fraction of what this country needs. It's as dry as a desert."

As they passed through a meadow, a dirty cloud hung against the side of a distant slope.

"Is that smoke?" Jennifer asked.

Nancy nodded. "The Forest Service is burning away some of the forest floor buildup. If you look between the big trees, there are a lot of fallen logs, small trees, and bushes so thick you can't see through them. If a fire starts in the forest, like from lightning, all that buildup burns really hot and lasts a long time. The hotter it burns and the longer, the more it creeps up the big trees to the branches and sets them on fire. At that point, you can have a monstrous fire.

"Well, if the forest floor didn't have that buildup, the fire would sweep through quickly, burning only the pine needles and leaves and other small stuff between the trees and not burning long enough to affect the big trees. It's a self-cleaning action. So the Forest Service picks different areas and deliberately starts small fires to burn the heavy stuff on the ground. Those fires are called 'controlled burns'."

"Isn't that kind of dumb?" Jennifer asked. "I mean, if it gets out of control, doesn't it act just like a regular forest fire?"

"Yes," Nancy said. "It's difficult, but there are methods to keep a controlled burn contained. The fire crews work hard to make sure it doesn't get away from them. The burn producing the smoke that you see has already been a problem. It got away from them early yesterday morning, and they had to bring in an extra Forest Service crew to get it back under control. I've heard that it's going much better today.

"Having a clean forest floor can make a world of difference in terms of permanent damage to a whole forest, so I think it's worth it. Before people started managing the forests and believed that fires were always bad, the forest floor was kept clean by the occasional fires that occurred naturally.

"Controlled burns are becoming so important that we're thinking about putting a Fire Day into our program activities, which would include a tour of burned and unburned areas, plus a visit with a fire management crew to see their operations. Doing those burns is one of the biggest environmental issues in this area."

The dirty cloud went out of sight as they rounded a curve. Mogi kept looking through the forest, noticing the thick undergrowth that Nancy had talked about. If a fire started in that mess, he didn't see how you could control anything.

* * *

Nancy, Mogi, and Jennifer went through the door marked Staff Only and took an elevator to the second floor. Nancy had stopped and gotten a cardboard box from her office at the lab, and Mogi carried it to the meeting. The conference room was small but not crowded, as the exhibit committee had only three members. An older man sat in a chair to the side of the conference table.

"Thank you for coming, Nancy," the committee chairman said. He introduced the others and then motioned to the older man. "We have a special guest, a most fortunate guest for this occasion. Let me introduce Alexander Soboknov. Dr. Soboknov is visiting from a Russian university, working with the laboratory's intelligence group. He saw the exhibit, was interested in knowing more, and offered to give a perspective we've never had.

"For starters, one of the men in the famous Soviet warehouse photograph is Dr. Soboknov's father."

Nancy's eyes grew wide at the introduction. She did not know the man and did not know of any Russian interest in the incident.

"I'll give an overview of the incident history," the chairman continued, "and that will be a good starting point for discussing the exhibit." He dimmed the lights and used his laptop and a projector to display images onto a screen.

"Some of these photos were Top Secret until they were declassified during the early 1990s." He pushed a button. The first image was of two planes in an airplane hangar surrounded by several men with dollies, boxes, and ropes. A couple of men were inspecting one of the planes. The chairman said they were Henry Samples and Christopher Johnson, the pilot and co-pilot.

"During the late evening of August 23rd and the early morning hours of August 24th, 1963, two identically marked, modified BeechCraft airplanes were used to move a special shipment of plutonium from Rocky Flats to Los Alamos. This is a picture of the two planes inside a hangar at a private airstrip on the north side of Denver.

"Consistent with their procedures at the time, one plane was loaded with two hundred pounds of refined plutonium metal, packed in six yellow, suitcase-sized containers. The other plane was loaded with six identical containers holding two hundred pounds of lead. No one at the scene could tell the true containers from the decoy containers. Supposedly, even the pilots of the airplanes did not know."

The image changed to show a set of yellow containers.

"At 1:45 a.m., the planes took off from the airstrip. Approximately two and a half hours later, at 4:07 a.m., over the Carson National Forest west of Tres Piedras, New Mexico, one of the planes lost altitude and crashed into dense trees."

A new photo showed wreckage in the middle of a charred area of forest.

"At the time the one plane crashed, the other airplane disappeared from radar. When that happened, Los Alamos officials monitoring the flight immediately scrambled two fighters out of Albuquerque, which was standard procedure. The jets spotted the burning wreckage of the first but failed to locate the second.

"It took another hour before an investigation crew on the ground could confirm that the downed plane carried the six containers of lead, increasing the urgency of the search for the second plane, the plane that was piloted by Samples and Johnson.

"The investigation was extended over the countryside, but was narrowed when reports were received from villagers along the north side of the Jemez Mountains, about sixty miles southwest of the crash site. A plane had been heard passing low overhead during the night. Within an hour, a makeshift landing strip was located halfway between Gallina and Coyote, two remote villages fifty air miles northwest of Los Alamos."

The man displayed a map marked with the landing strip and then changed the image to a long and relatively flat pasture. A long line of white stakes about twenty yards apart marked the side of the field.

"Lanterns were used to mark the pasture for a night landing, and several sets of tire tracks were found, including tracks that matched the tires of the airplane. However, no vehicles, plane, or other evidence were at the field when it was discovered.

"There was no communication with the second plane after it disappeared from radar. However, at approximately 4:49 that morning, a series of what seemed to be Morse code signals were received at the Los Alamos airport. The airport dispatcher, who was skilled in Morse code, recognized no clear message. As was protocol, he recorded the various sounds in the dispatcher logbook."

A new image showed an airport dispatcher's logbook, with a close-up of an entry of scribbled dots and dashes. Mogi had learned Morse code in the Boy Scouts but did not recognize any meaningful sequence of dots or dashes.

"As there were no other planes in that airspace at the time, it was assumed that these signals came from the second plane. However, what at first looks like the dots and dashes of Morse code is, in fact, no message at all. The mysterious sequence made no sense, and after careful analysis, was judged to be a random event and probably a malfunction in the remote electric lines in the mountains, which were sometimes primitive at best.

"As was standard procedure with any transport of nuclear material, a crisis management team was immediately assembled to carry out an investigation. After two weeks of intense activity, all leading to nothing, an official board of inquiry was convened. The remote airstrip, the crash site of the first airplane, the pictures of the initial loading of the planes, the backgrounds of the pilots, the operations, the flight plan—every detail was examined.

"Within a month, the final judgment was that a deliberate and calculated action on the part of one or both pilots had been carried out. Since it was a top-secret operation as well as a government operation, the entire incident was classified, and no information about the real purpose of the airplanes was provided to the public. The fact that there were two planes, which was an ongoing security element to the transport of nuclear materials, was deleted from the final report.

"The next major development was five years later, with the appearance of a photograph that showed the six containers of plutonium in a Russian warehouse."

The man put up the picture that Mogi remembered from the exhibit—several men standing next to a forklift with the containers in the background. Nancy sat patiently, listening.

"It was intended as a coup on the part of the Soviet intelligence community. Based on this photograph, it was generally accepted that one or both of the pilots of the aircraft defected to the Soviet Union. The photograph, even though it was obviously leaked to the United States, provoked certain congressmen to demand action in the face of the Soviets' thumbing their nose at us.

"Following another internal investigation and lacking any evidence to the contrary, both pilots were judged as having committed high treason against the United States although all of those proceedings were classified as well. Using a military court instead of a civil court, the judgment resulted in full convictions of both men. The order for their convictions was signed by the president and stands to this day."

With this, the chairman turned up the lights and retook his seat at the table.

"All of this information, as I said, was declassified in the early 1990s. Beginning at that time and in response to several requests by Dr. Simpson, a full disclosure was made to her and her family regarding the investigations, and copies of all the pictures, documents, and reports were given to them.

"With regard to how the exhibit is purposed," the chairman said with a shrug, "our hands are pretty much tied by the official record."

He directed his attention to Dr. Soboknov, who had watched intently during the presentation.

"Dr. Soboknov, we've never had any knowledge of the Soviet side of this incident. Is there anything you can share with us?"

The older man cleared his throat. "I wish I could," he began in a soft voice, "but your slides have shown me more than what I knew. Even though my father worked in the warehouse, he, of course, would never have known the history of the containers. I'm sure, as are you, that the photograph was staged. My father was probably just a handy individual they placed in the picture to make it look real."

His voice was deep and rich, with a thick accent. He slowly stood and addressed the others in an awkward, formal way.

"It has been only in the last few years that I learned about the incident and have kept only a personal interest in the details. Through some informal inquiries—you have to remember that Russia is not yet quite as open with their history as you are—I have found few additional details.

"Yes, there was some sort of intelligence operation to intercept the plutonium. There was at least one member of the ground crew working with the planes who was a Soviet agent. I have heard only that the results of the attempt are still classified, but the general belief is that it was successful. Yes, the containers in the warehouse certainly look real although even we laugh at the idea that containers containing plutonium would actually be kept on a shelf in a warehouse. And, yes, I'm not likely to find out any more."

The other men chuckled at his last comment. Cold war or no cold war, nations would never abandon their desire for secrets.

"So, I am not much help," the Russian continued, "although I wish very much that I could provide more facts about the pilot and co-pilot. In particular, I do not know if they were our agents, nor if their names were ever recorded anywhere in Soviet documents."

He turned to Nancy and said apologetically, "Very few people are still alive who could provide me with the information. I am sorry. I wish I could do more." He sat down.

It was now Nancy's turn.

"I've discussed this with laboratory officials through the years," she said as she leaned forward on the table, "and I believe that all of you are aware of my arguments. However," she nodded to Dr. Soboknov, "I'll cover the most important points again.

"First, the cover story created for the public was that there was one plane that had crashed because of engine trouble; there was no second plane. With the invention of that story and keeping all the information classified, the government prevented any additional information from being gathered from area villagers or other possible witnesses. In particular, the villagers were no longer questioned about what they heard or about the landing site. No questions about the second plane, no questions about the vehicles that left the tracks, no questions about any comings or goings before or after the incident.

"It is my position that, as soon as the government found a way to bury the story, they stopped looking for anything else. The government was terribly embarrassed by losing the plutonium, and once it seemed that it was a hijacking by the Russians, it was more desirable to get the incident over quickly, rather than do a thorough job of investigating. In short, having defined the truth for their convenience, they then acted as if it were the truth."

No expressions changed on the faces of the committee members.

"Secondly, performing a conviction *in absentia*, and the fact that it was done by a military court, violated my father's rights as a non-military participant. It was a clear violation of his civil rights.

"And thirdly, there is one formal report that indicates that the Soviet Union never possessed the plutonium at all. It is the best confirmation of my own theory that the plutonium was never stolen in the first place. We may not know where it went, but it did not go to the Soviet Union."

This must be what she meant on the bus, Mogi thought.

"This formal report, which was not classified, was promptly dismissed by Pentagon officials and was removed from public access by the CIA."

Mogi was fascinated. This Dr. Simpson, the professional scientist, was considerably different from Nancy, the leader of a bunch of teen-agers who waded in streams after little fishies.

She talked for a few minutes more, filling in more details she'd learned over the years. The Russian professor was the kindest of the men in the room. The others showed little to no reaction though some remarks about the unofficial report seemed, to Mogi, to be mean-spirited.

Eventually, they got around to discussing what to do about the exhibit.

CHAPTER
5

"You knew they wouldn't change the exhibit, didn't you?" Jennifer asked as they left the museum.

"The ways of bureaucracy are strange," Nancy replied. "Once something has been stated officially, it's hard for people to even consider anything else, even if it was a stupid thing to say in the first place. I swear, if I hear one more bureaucrat tell me that his hands are tied, I'm going to rip his arms off." She smiled. "Not really. I should be used to it by now, I guess."

As they drove back to the mountains, Nancy continued, "My mother was told only that my dad's plane developed engine trouble and crashed. She was taken to the wreckage of the first plane and then, later, attended a funeral where a casket was buried with an unrecognizable body that supposedly was her husband.

"She was not aware of the second plane, nor of the mission of the plane, nor of the loss of the plutonium, nor of the warehouse photograph, nor even of my father's trial. People who believed my father had gotten a raw deal leaked the details around 1978. My mother asked for official inquiries, but there weren't many people interested anymore, especially not anyone who might be accused of bungling the situation. She died in 1980.

"When I came to the lab in 1990, I was active in getting the information released, including all of the photographs that you saw. I also saw the logbook for the first time, and, although I was not allowed to keep it, I was allowed to photocopy it.

"There were a few people still alive who were part of the operation, but I didn't find anyone who knew more than what I had uncovered officially. It's only by sheer luck that a friend of mine was working on assignment at the Pentagon, knew which questions to ask, and analyzed the situation for me. He produced the formal report I referred to."

"Is that the stuff from your investigation?" Mogi asked, pointing to the well-worn box he had carried to the meeting.

"Yes. I've kept a record of everything I've found. I expected I might have needed to produce some of the papers I've collected. However, as you saw, they were not really into arguing evidence. They already had their minds made up."

Mogi's face turned red. "Uh, well, would you mind. . .uh. . .if I looked over some of the. . .uh. . .your. . .stuff?"

"You think you can find something that I've missed?" Nancy said.

"Oh, uh. . .no, I'm just. . .uh. . .interested," he replied.

Jennifer laughed. "You'll have to pardon my dorky brother, Dr. Simpson. He can't help himself. When he smells anything like a mystery or a puzzle, his brain kind of switches tracks and he just has to play Sherlock Holmes. Fortunately, he's surprisingly good at it. If we ever have a few minutes to visit, I'll tell you about some of our adventures."

Nancy smiled. "Well, far be it for me to refuse Sherlock Holmes. Take the box and browse to your heart's content," she said to Mogi. "Just be careful, and don't lose anything."

The day was ending even better than he could have imagined, Mogi thought.

An almost-full moon changed the browns and greens of the forest into shades of black and silver. As they crossed over the pass, Mogi could see the distant lights of the conference center sparkle in a sea of gray.

Behind him, the dirty cloud of smoke still rose in the distance, a little larger than before.

*   *   *

The dorms of the conference center were more like hotels than other camps Mogi had been to, which made him happy—he had room to be alone. With twenty-four students in a dorm of a hundred rooms, there was no reason to double up. Mogi had one side of a two-bedroom suite, Pistol had the other side, and they shared a bathroom in between. Raymond Peña, who liked to be called Pistol, was from Page, Arizona.

Mogi took a blanket, smoothed it over the mattress of the second bed in his room, and removed everything from Nancy's box, organizing the items into neat piles. There were photographs, some of which he had already seen and some he had not, and a few court-like papers that looked like transcripts of a trial. There was a thick document that seemed to be a full account of the incident, a copy of the logbook from the airport dispatcher, a couple of timesheets, graphs with different activities in order of their occurrence, and a few envelopes with yet more papers, notes, and diagrams.

"Watcha doin'?" Pistol asked, strolling through the door from the bathroom.

"Careful with this stuff," he said as Pistol came near the bed, "and don't move anything. I'm working on a mystery."

"Hey, that's cool. What's the mystery?"

Mogi directed his suitemate into the desk chair, away from the bed. Using the notes he had typed into his phone at the meeting, he went through the story, trying to be as smooth as the guy at the museum. He used the same pictures, handing them to Pistol as he talked.

A few minutes after Mogi finished speaking, Pistol said, "Hello? Are you still here?"

"Oh, sorry." Mogi kept having moments when his voice drifted off and he found himself staring at the ceiling. Repeating the story made him think of more questions. If the second plane had crashed, it would have been found, eventually; therefore it didn't crash. If it didn't crash, how far could it have flown before it needed to be refueled? Did they refuel it at the makeshift airfield? Had the investigators checked for spilled fuel on the ground? If it continued flying, why didn't it show up on radar? Maybe there wasn't radar coverage in some areas, but wouldn't that tell you the direction the plane would have gone?

He was understanding Nancy's comment about the investigation not being done very well.

"You mean they convicted the guys without them even being there? That doesn't seem fair. What about the third guy?"

Mogi looked at him with a blank stare. "There were only two—the pilot and copilot. Samples and Johnson."

"Hand me that picture over there." Pistol took a photograph showing the plane in the hangar and held it close to his face. "Look. See right here. See the edges right here and along here. That's a hat. Somebody's inside the plane and he's wearing a hat, you know, like what old guys wear."

Mogi didn't want to look because it was a waste of time. There were only two men. If there had been more than two men, they would have talked about more than two men. But he looked, and then looked again, surprised. It *did* look like a hat.

"How'd you see that? I'm not sure that's anything. Maybe a shadow."

"No, dude, that's a hat. I've got pretty good eyes. My dad's always getting me to spot fish in the water when we're out on the lake. I'm good at looking for shapes."

Mogi looked intently at the photograph, moving it around, holding it directly under the light, comparing it to other photos. It did look like a hat or something; it was a couple of straight lines, at least. But that couldn't be. There was no mention anywhere about a third man. No one had been identified except Henry Samples and Christopher Johnson, and that's not something they would lie about.

"Uh, I'll have to ask Nancy about it, but I'm pretty sure there wasn't a third guy."

"Well, OK," Pistol said, "but that's still a hat."

Having finished what he remembered of the presentation, Mogi told Pistol about the meeting in town with Nancy and the committee.

"The guy's a spy," Pistol said matter-of-factly.

"Who's a spy?"

"The Russian professor. You think he just happened to show up? The exhibit is new, telling about spies and stolen plutonium, there's a special meeting to talk about it, and suddenly, a Russian shows up. No way is that an accident. I bet they're even watching you, dude."

"You're making that up. He didn't look like a spy. Seemed like a nice guy to me."

Pistol stood, leaned against the wall, and put his hands behind his head. "This is the way they operate. Trust me. I saw a program once about a spy who had been an ordinary guy for twenty years. Absolutely ordinary. Suddenly, he disappears from his job and the next week he shows up on Russian TV talking about all the secrets he'd been stealing the whole time.

"Now you've got missing plutonium and suddenly there's a Russian. Doesn't even seem real clever to me, but you watch to see if he doesn't start showing up more often. The guy's a spy. It happens on TV all the time. Coincidences. You've got to pay attention to coincidences." Pistol spoke with an air of confidence and finality.

The door in Pistol's room squeaked.

The two boys looked at each other. They got up and walked through the bathroom into the next room.

"Oh, man, I hope they didn't take anything," Pistol said, shuffling through his stuff. "I didn't close the door when I came to your room."

Mogi looked at the half-open door, slipped through, and looked into the hall. Empty.

Pistol was sniffing the air behind him. He walked up to Mogi and sniffed him up close.

"Well, it's not you. Must have been the ghost."

Mogi noticed the smell. It was aftershave lotion or cologne or deodorant or something. Whew. Way too strong.

Pistol hadn't found anything missing but was checking his closet just to be sure, so Mogi left him and walked back into his room. He pulled the chair up close to the blanket-draped mattress and carefully browsed again through each pile of Nancy's stuff.

He found the report about the Soviets not having the plutonium at all. After the Soviet Union broke up and the United States was helping Russia manage their warheads, the history of Soviet atomic bomb development came to light, including how many had been manufactured. Nancy's friend had counted the Soviet weapons made after 1963. If the Soviet Union suddenly had gained two hundred extra pounds of unexpected plutonium, there would have been a sudden jump in the number or the size of the bombs they'd made.

But there wasn't. No change at all which, in Nancy's mind, said that they never had the plutonium to begin with.

Mogi packed all the materials neatly back into the box and tucked it into the corner of his closet, hiding it under a towel. Locking the doors to his room, he went out the back door of the dorm, followed the access road around a second dorm, and stepped onto the ranch's main road.

It was 9:30 on a quiet, cool evening in the mountains.

He walked to the corrals, stopped for a moment to gaze at the horses, and then went past the big log house. The road crossed over a cattle guard and became dirt as it continued across a pasture. A heavy gate made of thick metal pipe hung across the cattle guard.

Mounting the bottom pipe, Mogi kicked off with his foot and the gate slowly swung open. Switching sides, the heavy pipe gate carried him back. As the gate clicked back into its catch, he climbed to the top rail and sat, looking back at the ranch. The moonlit expanses of grass looked like silver carpet, rolling up and down with little bumps and valleys until it dissolved into the black line of forest. He took a deep breath and tasted the aroma of the grass and the forest.

What a world it must have been, he thought. Big bombers up in the sky every day, every night, every minute, loaded with nuclear weapons, flying twenty-four hours a day, every day, waiting. Waiting in case the Soviet Union should attack. Waiting to strike back or, if they had to, to strike first.

Hundreds of silos with missiles fueled and ready to launch at the flick of a switch. A network of radar sites stretching across Canada. Submarines with missiles that had nuclear warheads, cruising invisibly all over the world. Spies in every country.

Everybody watching everybody else. One flinch and the whole world gets blown to smithereens.

Then the world finally got smarter. The wall in Berlin came down, the Soviet Union disbanded, Russia held elections, and both nations started dismantling their warheads.

Who would want plutonium now? Somebody who wanted their own nuclear weapons, like Iraq, Iran, North Korea, just for starters. From the posters at the museum, it took a lot of effort to make plutonium, and that's why a lot of countries hadn't even tried. But if you already had it, making it blow up might not be too hard.

The question wasn't really meant to be serious, but Mogi's mind worked on it anyway.

Terrorists might want some. Libyans, Syrians, Al Qaeda, ISIS. They'd love to have a nuclear weapon, but just having any radioactive material might serve them as well. Blow up a regular bomb surrounded with the stuff in New York City and some neighborhoods might be uninhabitable for centuries.

And crazy people. Crazy people might want a few pounds of plutonium to do crazy things with.

Then there were the people who wouldn't want to use it, but to sell it. How much would two hundred pounds of plutonium be worth?

Mogi thought about Pistol's spy theory. If the photograph of the cases in Russia was a fake and they never actually had the stuff, then it was still out there somewhere. Two hundred pounds of plutonium might be worth waiting for—and watching out for—even after all these years. It would certainly be worth sending another spy over to keep up with developments, especially if he looked like an old, friendly, innocent bystander.

Mogi's hands were getting cold from holding onto the metal gate railing. He climbed down and headed back to the center.

CHAPTER

I t was late, but Mogi knew that his brain was in high gear. It would take a while for his inner voices to quiet down enough for him to sleep, so he took the long way to the dorm, passing by the loading dock of the dining hall, across the auditorium steps, around the side, and across the parking lot. On the south side of the auditorium building was the equipment room. A large garage door was open and light spilled out across the asphalt.

Mogi cautiously walked up and peeked in. There were lots of backpacks hanging from the walls and long lines of sleeping bags suspended from the ceiling. Around the room were shelves full of sleeping pads, backpacking stoves, axes, tents, canned food, and all sorts of other camping equipment.

A couple of older teen-agers, also summer assistants, were sorting through packages and boxes on two large tables near the door.

"Come on in, if you want to look around," one of them called. "We're just sorting equipment and making a few repairs."

Mogi slid his way through the door, trying to be invisible.

The room was stuffed with equipment—hooks and hangers, shelves and boxes, labels and signs were everywhere. Every cubby hole was filled with something, and every place a hook could be screwed into the wall was hung with materials. Mogi listened as the two boys talked about the latest backpacking trip. If half of what they said were true, it was going to be the best activity of all. Mogi had backpacked as a boy scout, but most trips were in the Utah canyon country; only once had he made a weekend trek into high mountains.

He walked between the rows of packs and sleeping bags. A small room was tucked into the back corner, its door ajar. Mogi glanced to see if anyone was inside and then pushed the door open.

It was an office, with an old wooden desk against a wall, a wooden, rolling chair drawn up to it, windows into the storage area, and a filing cabinet to the side. Half the room was caged off, like a big locker or something, with wire mesh welded onto a steel frame that went floor to ceiling. There was a mesh door, latched by a big lock hanging from a clasp.

Cautiously stepping through the door, he peered through the mesh. Big bags hung from long wire hooks. Several boxes were on the floor, some stacked, others bunched up against each other. On a shelf were two pairs of boots. Not regular boots, but big, thick-soled leather boots, the leather creased and worn, almost knee height, with lots of holes for laces. To the left hung a couple of huge, pullover-type, full-length body suits, heavily padded and thick, with big pockets across the legs and chest.

He looked across the front of the cage and followed the wall around the desk.

Photographs. Maybe fifty, taped all over the walls, next to the door, over the desk, on the filing cabinets, around the edge of the lamp. Some were old, he could tell, because they were small and the edges were curled. Others were larger, and several were in panoramic formats. He leaned forward for a closer look.

Mountain peaks. Billowing clouds of smoke and flames.

The pictures were of forest fires, some taken really close up and some taken above the fires, obviously from an airplane, or maybe a drone? Some pictures had groups of people gathered in parking lots with backpacking gear, others had only one or two people, either in parkas, climbing gear, or in bright yellow shirts.

Nancy.

Mogi leaned forward to look at the photograph taped on the wall to his right. It was Nancy! She looked younger, but there was no mistaking the smile. A man stood with his arm around her shoulders.

Whose office was this, anyway?

He jumped about a foot when the noise of a closing garage door rattled through the big room.

Mogi was off in a flash, barely making it outside before the garage door settled against the cement floor. The two staffers hadn't even remembered he was there.

*   *   *

The controlled burn—the one producing the smoke Mogi noticed on the way to town—was set on Sunday morning by workers at Bandelier National Monument, next to LANL land and bordering some of the Valles Caldera Preserve, all of which were part of the Jemez Mountain range. Everything was going well until Sunday afternoon when the fire spread across the forest floor faster than expected, at which time a fire-fighting crew was requested from the National Forest Service.

The crew calmed it down, got it back inside the planned perimeter, and everything returned to normal. The regular Bandelier forest crew went about their business of burning more of the underbrush. With the drop of temperature that night, the flames stayed close to the ground and calmly burned through the undergrowth.

Tuesday morning, gusty winds increased the fire's radius, and it again jumped outside its planned perimeter. The gusts acted like a fan, blowing the small fires into big fires, and the flames grew enough to race up the tall trees and ignite the upper limbs full of thick needles and pinecones, the "crowns" of the trees. With the flames now shooting above the trees, whole clouds of sparks were caught in the wind gusts and swept into the forest of a nearby slope. The fire soon doubled in size and was far beyond what a local fire management crew could handle.

The fire was declared out of control at about 4 o'clock on Tuesday afternoon.

At that point, the Bandelier officials notified the National Forest Service, which sent in several fire-fighting units from the surrounding towns. After short-term measures did not bring the fire under control by evening, the Forest Service's Central Fire Management Office in Grand Junction, Colorado, was notified of the situation and assumed authority over the blaze.

Because the fire was so close to a national monument, a national preserve, and a town, the fire was declared a "priority fire" and a special command center was created for managing everyone and everything that would be brought in to fight the fire.

Everything was in motion, but it wasn't until late Tuesday evening that Jim Daniels drove into the mountains, having been dispatched out of Grand Junction. Jim was named the incident commander and would be responsible for directing the firefighters around the edges of the fire, laying out the paths of the monstrous bulldozers, calling in planes to dump fire retardant if they were needed, managing the helicopters that would dump water, and a hundred other things.

Jim had fought hundreds of wildland fires all across the states, including Alaska. He'd been a bulldozer operator, he'd parachuted into remote areas as a "smokejumper," and he'd served on "hotshot" crews for years. An elite firefighter, he felt ready for whatever might happen.

Reading the most recent reports from the crews, Jim was not overly concerned and expected that this fire could be handled with only the fire crews, hotshots, and a couple of bulldozers. The fire was miles away from any buildings, several logging roads provided good access, and the cool nighttime temperatures of the mountains would be a natural damper to the flames.

His biggest worry was the wind. The weather people had identified two quickly-moving fronts set to collide over the Arizona–New Mexico border. It was possible that a narrow channel of air might start forming across the Southwest with gusts at thirty to fifty miles an hour, but it was hard to guess at what altitude. It was also too early to tell whether or not its path would include the Jemez Mountains.

If the channel came too close to the fire, fast winds would act like a bellows across the burning coals of a forge, and fighting the fire would become an exercise in trying to snuff out a blowtorch.

If the direction of the wind changed to the northwest, it was going to blow flames and sparks and embers across the rugged face of the eastern slopes of the Jemez Mountains. These slopes not only had a hundred years worth of tall pine, spruce, fir, and aspen, but a crowded, untouched, and extremely dry forest floor.

All of it surrounded Los Alamos National Laboratory and a city of seventeen thousand people.

But today's problems were enough for now. Jim casually wrote out orders for ten more fire crews, ten more teams of hotshots, and two bulldozers to begin as soon as daybreak. He was going to cut a fire line on the north side of the fire and, if it held, he might have the fire under control before the wind became a problem.

By nine o'clock the next morning, Wednesday, he had gotten all of the fire crews on their lines, had sent the bulldozers to widen the roads and cut breaks, and had given his first briefing to the Forest Service personnel. The fire had quieted down as expected, and Jim was optimistic.

CHAPTER

Wednesday morning was Ranch Day for Mogi's team. It was a beautiful day, with a light breeze bringing moisture from the pastures and balancing the warmth of the morning sun.

After breakfast, Mogi's team collected their daypacks and headed for the corral. Several horses were saddled and tied to the corral posts. A tall, muscular man came around the corner of the barn, pushed open the barn door, and called for the group to move inside.

Mogi recognized the man—he was in the fire photographs Mogi had seen the night before. It must have been his office that Mogi had found.

Nancy walked ahead of the group and gave the man a big hug.

"Well, Nancy," the man said with a big grin, "I believe that my soul has been awakened by a hug like that!"

She looked up at him and smiled. "Well, Muck, I had forgotten how good looking you are and how you dazzle us young ladies with a mere flash of your smile!"

The man roared a full-bodied laugh. He was older than Nancy, for sure, Mogi thought, but it was hard to tell how old he was. He was lean and moved smoothly as he walked, like an athlete. His hair had a lot of gray, his skin was lined and tanned, and his hands were large, his fingers thick. His eyes lit up as he talked and highlighted a broad expanse of wonderfully white teeth. The man gathered the students around him.

"I want to welcome you to the ranch operations. My name is Muck Jones, and I'm the foreman of the ranch. It's my responsibility to make sure that everything that gets up in the morning gets back down at night, whether it be men, women, horses, cattle, or tractors."

He talked freely and confidently. He was funny and full of information about the ranch, the people, the animals, and everything else. He was like a Tonight Show entertainer rolled together with a genuine, cattle-pushing cowboy. He led them through the barn, explained the proper saddling techniques for the horses they would be riding, talked about the grazing procedures for the cattle, pointed out the ranch operations as they overlooked the different buildings, and then led them into the main house, a sprawling, two-story log home.

Mogi couldn't help but notice that Phil was making himself almost invisible. On Rock Day and River Day, he had been a constant pest to the team, casually insulting them when Nancy was occupied somewhere else, criticizing the way people took notes or wrote data, and wandering off when his help would actually have been appreciated. Today, though, he was clearly hiding at the back of the group and never said a word.

They stepped up onto the long porch and entered the house. Mogi liked that the log home was made with real logs, big and long, carefully notched and stacked on top of each other, and buffed to a shiny, dark brown finish.

"The center of the ranch operations, as one might expect, is the kitchen," Muck said as they walked through a large entry room into the kitchen. It was unbelievably huge, Mogi thought, with cabinets and workspaces along the outer walls and a big center island. There were three ovens and an eight-burner stove along the far wall, as well as two full refrigerators and a freezer.

"When the camp was in its heyday—when a lot of timber was being trucked out of here and over ten thousand cattle were pastured during the summers—about forty-five men would take their daily meals here. There'd be forty steaks, half-a-bushel of potatoes, two gallons of gravy, three cakes, and ten pies spread all over the table, and that was just lunch," Muck said with a grin and a laugh.

Next to the kitchen was a dining room that was forty feet long, with a single huge table from end to end. Along the table were chairs made of rustic wood, their seats and backs covered with cowhide. Double doors led into a room the size of a dance hall, filled with round tables and chairs, a few sofas, and a large TV. Past that room were bathrooms, storage rooms, pantries, a utility room, and a handsomely crafted staircase up to the second floor, which held several bedrooms and another bathroom.

Muck explained that the walls, floor, and ceiling planks, the table, the chairs, and the fireplace stone had all come from the ranch property. The ranch had even built its own sawmill to cut the logs to lumber.

"Why don't we get to stay here?" one of the students asked.

"Why? I can tell you why," Muck said. "Sprinklers! The government said we had to put fire sprinklers in here and all over the rest of the house if it was going to be a 'public building.' And we'd have to redo all the bathrooms for handicap access, and put in an elevator.

"Now, that's the government for you. This lodge has been operating just fine for decades, but somebody sits in Washington and decides that it doesn't fit their standards, and even if it doesn't improve anything about how the building operates, we have to spend a few million dollars just to fix it up. Well, it was cheaper to build a whole new complex of buildings than to remodel this one house."

Muck was well into a ten-minute rant on the evils of Washington bureaucrats when Nancy motioned to him. He stopped with a grin and led the group outside and back to the stables.

Each student was taken to a horse that was saddled. Mogi's horse was large, solid brown, and didn't pay much attention as he lifted himself up and into the saddle. Mogi had been on a horse when he was young, but had sat behind his father. He was now much taller but found the saddle awkward and uncomfortable; he knew his back would be hurting by the end of the day.

A little nervous, he knew the general idea was to give little kicks with his heels when he wanted to go, and to pull back on the reins when he wanted to stop. Once the group started out of the corral, though, no matter what Mogi did, the horse ignored him. Used to the routine, the horse fell into a pace behind the others as they were led out of the stable area and across the pastures to the edge of the forest.

After about an hour, Mogi finally relaxed and fell into the rhythm of the horse and was able to focus on the forest around him. The smell was wonderful, rich and full with a heavy smell of pine trees. It reminded him of fresh Christmas trees when they were first brought into the house.

Muck Jones rode a beautiful black horse at the front of the line. Sitting tall and easy, he led the band of adventurers into a small canyon. At his direction, the teens stopped their horses, with more falling off than actually dismounting. They tied the reins to trees or logs and gathered behind a rock outcropping. A thick canvas bag carried by a packhorse was brought out and, to their great delight, Nancy distributed sack lunches. An insulated bag of drinks was put in the center of the group, and everyone made a grab for what they wanted.

While the group ate, Nancy talked about the ecology of the forest they had come through—the different trees, grasses, and bushes and the various foods they provided for animals; the wetness of the floor environment, resulting from the thickness of the pine needles, pine cones, and bark and how it all decomposed to make natural fertilizer; and the natural protection the forest provided for both animals and vegetation.

Muck followed, sounding like a forest ranger. He talked about the forest's large animals, such as elk, deer, and bear: their behavior patterns, where and what they found for food, and the need for having a large preserve to keep them active and healthy.

As he gave his talk, Muck used every opportunity to give short sermons about the failings of the National Forest Service, the National Park Service, the Bureau of Land Management, and the government in general. None of Muck's stories were mean and most were humorous, filled with his personal encounters with the local arms of these organizations.

After cleaning their lunch area, even to the point of sweeping their tracks with fallen pine branches, the students-becoming-scientists mounted up. The wind had picked up from the morning, and as they mounted and rode out of the canyon, a stiff breeze had Mogi keeping his windbreaker zipped up and his ball cap pulled low.

Muck led them up a steep trail. Mogi felt his horse change pace, slowing down but bearing more on his hind legs to power up the incline. He let the horse have his way and hung onto the saddle horn to keep from sliding out of the saddle. After an hour of climbing, the horses broke out of the thick trees and Mogi could see that they were close to the summit of the mountain in front of them. They had been climbing the tallest peak in the preserve and now stood directly above the conference center far below. It was a remarkable view.

With the wind now snapping at them, Muck maneuvered them into the protected side of a hill. Everyone welcomed the relief of getting out of the saddle although Muck made them double-check the way they tied their reins to an old log. It would be a long walk back if a horse came untied and went to the corral without its rider.

Muck arranged the teens in a half-circle and offered another round of drinks. He stood for a minute looking across the expansive pastures of the preserve and to the mountains in the east.

What had looked like a small thundercloud of a summer storm was now a dark column of smoke that towered up from the ground and broadened out into the wind, making a tail that blotted out the horizon.

"Tell me what you see," Muck said.

"Smoke!"

"Uh, it's a fire."

"It's a lot bigger than it was this morning."

"It looks like it's blowing away from us."

"I don't see any flames, so is it already out?"

Muck took a map from his daypack and spread it on the ground in front of the students. "The fire was a controlled burn set by the Park Service on Sunday morning for the purpose of burning the stored-up fire load on the forest floor, and it was started right here," Muck said, pointing to the map. "It was meant to burn in this direction," he said, using a pen to draw an arrow from the starting point, "and a smaller fire would be set down here." He drew a different arrow.

"It was intended to burn upwards this way and meet the main fire, which would then cause both fires to go out, since all the fuel would have been burned." He drew a squiggly line back to the start point. "However, they didn't count on the thickness of the undergrowth, nor the steepness of the slopes of the canyon below the fire area, which they should have expected, but didn't, since most of them are inexperienced and don't know what they're doing," Muck said in a matter-of-fact voice.

"So, instead of moving around this mountain, the sparks spread the fire to the forest below." He drew little arrows across the map. "And now they have a problem."

Mogi listened as if Muck Jones was a general briefing his troops.

He described how forest fires were fought, how hotshot crews were sent in to clean the forest debris out of the way so the fire had no material to burn. If the fire was in a remote area, special firefighters called smokejumpers parachuted from airplanes to do the same thing.

Bulldozers gouged roads through the trees and opened wide areas to keep the fire from spreading while tanker planes dropped tons of fire retardant in front of the fire's edges. Smaller fires, called backfires, would be lit to burn up the fuel before the main fire reached a certain location.

Mogi thought about having a forest fire back home. On the windswept and bare-rock landscape of southern Utah, a forest fire was the least of their worries. There was nothing to burn.

CHAPTER

"Do you think it was a third guy?"
Nancy looked through her reading glasses at the
photograph.

"Hmm. . .maybe. I'm not sure. I can't imagine a third person never being mentioned in the investigations or the trial."
She put the photograph on the table, leaned over, and folded
her hands while she stared at the shadow in the cockpit.

It was before supper, and the teen-agers crowded together
as the food line opened. The ranch group had been late coming
down the mountain so were just now making it to the dining
hall. The wind had gotten worse, and Muck was afraid of being
caught by tree limbs blown down across the trails. He'd led the
group out into the meadows, making for a longer trip home.

"On the other hand, if there had been a third person in the
plane," Nancy said, "it may not have been mentioned if that
person was with an organization that didn't exist."

In response to Mogi and Jennifer's puzzled expressions, she
continued.

"We currently live in a remarkably free climate for information, and we know a lot about the CIA, the NSA, the FBI,
the Delta Force, the SEALs, Area 51, and other government
operations. Movies go to great lengths to expose how secret

units operate and even show the details of events that were classified just a few months before, like the movie about killing Osama Bin Laden.

"But in the '60s, it was strictly forbidden to acknowledge that some organizations even existed. The United States could not have operated without secret organizations, and hiding their participation even within a classified event like the hijacking of plutonium could have been normal procedure."

"But if there were three people instead of two people, then somebody's lying," Mogi said with a sigh of exasperation. He slapped his hand against the table. "Somebody is lying! Somebody is lying, and we ought to find out who!"

Nancy tilted her head a little and leaned closer to him. "I think we should call this off," she said, looking into his face. "You're getting too wrapped up in it. I shouldn't have made such a fuss in the first place.

"I want you to stop thinking about the hijacking," she said. "Give it up. Even if we knew all the answers, it probably wouldn't be much more than what we already know."

"But it matters to you, doesn't it?" Mogi felt like a fool. He had not only failed to help with the problem, but he was making a nuisance of himself.

"Sure, it matters to me. But life goes on, and I go on, too. So you need to forget about all of this. Bring back my box and enjoy the rest of the week. Learn something new! This week ought to be an adventure, not an exercise in trying to solve old problems."

*   *   *

Supper was probably the same good food as usual, but Mogi ate quickly and was too distracted to notice. He really wanted to talk to Jennifer and make some kind of protest, but she and some others had joined up to play games in the recreation room. She consoled him a bit, but agreed that Mogi ought to pay attention to the program and stop trying to solve the mystery. He needed to enjoy himself.

Nice idea, he thought as he went back to his room. He knew why Nancy had said what she said, and he'd take back her box like she'd asked, but he didn't want to quit. He had gotten involved, and everything in him resisted giving up. If only people wouldn't lie about things. What good is information if you don't know if it's true or not? How can you put together a puzzle if someone refuses to give you all the pieces?

What if there was never any plutonium at all? What if the yellow cases were all fake? What if the plutonium had already been stolen, and the planes were a cover-up? What if somebody had lied? What if everybody had lied? What if it was all a vicious game?

Mogi got up, put on his jacket, and quietly closed the door behind him, hoping to leave without Pistol noticing.

Walking quickly across the parking lot, he crept into the equipment room unnoticed, slipping under the big door and through the mass of sleeping bags as the staffers were again sorting through piles of equipment. They were getting ready for Mountain Day in the morning.

The tiny office was still empty. He quietly entered and pushed the door almost closed behind him.

In the canyons behind his house in Bluff, Mogi had found an ancient Indian ruin. Tucked in the back of an alcove high in a canyon wall of solid sandstone, ancient cliff dwellers had built a series of stone huts. For seven or eight hundred years, the walls of rock and mud were hidden until, on a lucky bike ride through the canyon, Mogi had discovered them.

As exciting as it had been to explore the ruins, the real find was an opening in the back wall of the alcove that led to a small, almost circular crack in the stone wall of the canyon that opened to the sky a couple of hundred feet above. With a flat floor of sand, surrounded by towering walls of sandstone, Mogi found a place away from the world, a place of wonder, a place that was his. For thinking, for dreaming, for whatever he wanted.

But he wasn't in Utah. He wasn't able to be alone here unless he could get away from everything. He needed to be alone so he could sort through the information inside his head.

That's when he thought of the office. The photographs were no accident. They were there because someone had created a special place for his or her body and mind. Maybe he could kind of, well, borrow somebody else's special place for a while. To sit and to think.

And there was the picture of Nancy—he wanted to see that picture again.

As he sat in the chair, leaning closely to see the images of Nancy and Muck, the door suddenly slammed open, a body zoomed through the door, and a long arm slammed into Mogi's neck, forcing his face down onto the desk.

"Well, well, if it isn't the dweeb," a voice said close to Mogi's ear.

"You're all mine now," Phil whispered.

It had been a terrible day for fighting a forest fire.

What the weather people had feared came true: The colliding weather fronts produced a channel of strong winds shooting across Arizona and New Mexico. Making it worse, by mid-morning, the channel shifted directly toward the Jemez Mountains, which caught the slow-moving fire and kicked it into high gear, eating a wide swath through ten miles of forest and canyon on the west end of Bandelier National Monument.

The good news was that it hadn't burned to the north, so the highway from Los Alamos into the Jemez was still available for moving fire crews and equipment into the burning areas. The bad news was that the west end of Bandelier consisted of deep canyons that had no access—no roads for vehicles and no paths for fire crews. All Jim Daniels could do was watch the devastation from a helicopter.

As the fire grew during the day, Jim and his management people waged war against a merciless enemy, fighting desperately while evolving their strategies for the battles that were yet to come. They shuffled more fire crews and hotshots and then called for air support. Five big tankers with fire retardant started dropping loads into the forest in the afternoon, flanking the fire to keep it going south and east while crews set backfires along the highway.

It was a struggle that Jim was not winning.

CHAPTER

9

Mogi could do nothing but squirm.

"Whatcha doin' here, Franklin? Looks to me like you're stealin' stuff."

"I'm. . .not. . .doing. . .anything," Mogi managed to force out.

Phil pressed all of his weight on Mogi's back, his arm across Mogi's neck. Reaching down, he grabbed Mogi's arm, twisted it around behind him, and leaned his face close to Mogi's ear.

"Oh, yeah, I think you are. I think you're a thief, sneakin' in here to go through the desk, or maybe you're waiting for the rest of us to leave so you can make off with one of the sleeping bags, huh?"

The smell. Some sort of aftershave, cologne, or deodorant. Way too strong.

The smell that was in Pistol's room last night.

"Come on, Phil. I. . .wasn't. . .wasn't doing. . .anything!"

"Sappy little kid, ya runt! I think you need a lesson." Phil let up on Mogi's neck and slid him off the desk and out of the chair. Twisting his arm even more, he forced Mogi into a kneeling position, his forehead about an inch above the cement floor. "You need a good lesson."

Mogi felt pressure against his windpipe and discovered that he couldn't breathe.

But suddenly, the pressure let up. Someone had pulled Phil off Mogi and threw him to the floor.

Mogi looked up to see Muck Jones towering above him. "Speaking of lessons, you don't learn yours very well, do you, Phil?"

Phil scrambled to his feet. A couple of inches taller than Muck, he tried to look down at him but couldn't hold it. He shifted around on his feet.

"Ah, Muck, I was, uh, havin' some fun with the boy," Phil said as his voice quivered. "Wasn't goin' to hurt him. But I did catch him going through your desk, Muck. He's a little thief!"

"Get out of here, Phil," Muck said with a calm voice. "We're going to have another one of our talks in the morning, but I believe that you may have used up your last measure of grace."

Phil tried to look innocent, but his face turned into a scowl. He turned and stalked through the door.

Mogi rolled over into a sitting position and struggled to his feet. His arm hurt like crazy.

He hung his head. "I'm. . .uh, sorry. . .I was, uh. . .looking at your. . .uh, photographs."

"Lots of memories in these old pictures," Muck said as he ran his hand up and down Mogi's arm, testing the joints and the tendons. "You still have pain here? Feel anything when I press on it?"

Muck's hands were firm but gentle, and his fingers were twice the thickness of Mogi's own fingers. "Uh, nah. It hurts a little, but it'll be okay."

"Bring in a chair, and I'll tell you about some of these pictures."

Mogi hesitated, pretty sure that he was about to get a lecture on stealing or something; it might not go on so long if he were standing. Still, he got a folding chair, set it inside the room, and sat opposite Muck, not looking up.

"I'm sorry about Phil. I thought he was picking up on what we do around here, but it doesn't look like it."

"It's OK," Mogi said. "He's just a jerk."

"Well, it goes against what we're trying to teach, and I don't need somebody behaving badly. Of course, when he first came, he was making everybody do push-ups, so he's at least gotten a little better."

Mogi relaxed, looked up, and smiled. "I'm not very good at push-ups."

Muck settled into his office chair and, pointing to several of the photographs, talked about being a foreman at a ranch in northwestern Wyoming. Besides raising cattle, there was a dude ranch business on the side, and he was hired to create a youth program to go with the adult programs.

"We did a lot of backpacking, mountain climbing, rock climbing, and stuff. We'd drive to the Wind River Range and pack in for a week at a time, or go over to Yellowstone for a weekend. That's where I met Nancy. She was working with the Forest Service in Yellowstone, collecting data on the buffalo herds and studying how they shared territory with the elk and bears. Those were pretty good days," he said as he leaned back in the chair.

"Well," Muck finally said. "I've got to help my staffers get ready for tomorrow, so I'll just apologize again and leave it at that. Ol' Phil never has figured out that real leadership is serving others, helping others to be leaders themselves, and not demanding to be the boss all the time."

He leaned over, gave a little laugh, and looked into Mogi's eyes.

"Real leadership is listening and understanding, helping people figure out how they fit in, what they can do, and then letting them do it. That's why we put the teams into situations where everybody kind of sorts themselves into what they can contribute. Leadership isn't about promoting an individual into a superior position over others. It's about developing the skills that allow team members to function in a smart way."

*   *   *

Mogi was soon back in the dorm hallway, wishing Muck had had more time—he had a way of telling stories that made every word worth listening to.

Unlocking the door and walking through the door of his dorm room, Mogi froze.

That smell.

This time he knew exactly where it had come from. Mogi's eyes darted around the room. Phil must have a key. What had he done?

Nancy's box!

He jumped across the room and pulled the box out of the closet. Something was different. Photographs, documents, manila envelopes, photocopies—the number of things, the thickness, the order.

The order—things were out of order.

As he'd laid the contents of the box on the bed the night before, he had straightened the edges of stacked papers, smoothed creased pages, ordered the envelopes by size, and put everything back into the box neatly. Now as he looked into the box, he could see that some of the pages had been jammed back in. The largest manila folder was on top of a smaller one. He wouldn't do that. Largest always went on the bottom.

He carefully spread the items on the extra bed.

One photograph was gone: The photograph of the two planes in the hangar, with Henry Samples and Chris Johnson standing in various piles of clutter while the planes were being loaded.

A shudder went up Mogi's spine and up through his neck. Sweat beaded on his forehead and his stomach muscles twisted. He had promised Nancy that he would take care of everything.

He made doubly sure, placing every item on the bed like he remembered, comparing his mental picture of every piece of information, every picture, and every document. After a few minutes, he was sure that Phil had taken only the one picture. If that was so, it was a photograph other people had—the museum, for one—so it could be replaced. Nothing had been lost.

He took a deep breath and wheeled the chair over to the desk. Phil could have taken the whole box, but he took only one photograph, a big one, one that he was sure Mogi would notice.

So, Phil wasn't stealing anything in particular. It was just a taunt—a finger in the chest, a tweak of the nose. It was just Phil being Phil—a one hundred percent jerk. It must have been Phil who'd been in Pistol's room. He heard all the stuff that Mogi talked about and knew that it had come from the box. Tonight, having just suffered embarrassment by Muck's appearance, he must have wanted to punish Mogi. But why the box? Phil was usually more direct: slapping the head, spilling Mogi's drink in the dining hall, pushing or shoving him whenever he was close. Getting something from the box seemed one step closer to making things personal.

Well, OK, enough of Phil.

Mogi hadn't gotten his private time in Muck's office like he'd wanted, which meant he hadn't gotten all of his thinking done, which meant he was still as wired tonight as he was last night, which meant he needed to get to work.

The box's contents were still spread across the blanket.

He wheeled his chair next to the bed and carefully went over each item again. If you don't know the whole picture, he thought, you look at each piece for what it can tell you. Look at each piece as if you're listening to it, as if it were something asking to be discovered.

He opened the logbook to the page with the dots and dashes. Even though the airport dispatcher had written hurriedly, it was still easy to make out the difference between dots and dashes.

```
. . . . - - - . . - - . - . . - . . . . . . . . . . . . - . - .
. . . - . . . . - . . . . . - . - . - . . . . . . . . . . - . . .
. - - . . . - - - . - - - . . . . . . - . . . . . . - - - . - .
. - - . - . . - . . . . . . . . . . - . . - . . . . - . . . .
- . . . . - . - . - . . . . . . . . . - . . . . - - . . . - - -
. - - - . . . . . . - . . . . - - - . - . . - - . . . . - .
```

He remembered the Morse code basics: one to five dots or dashes stood for letters or numbers. In Boy Scouts, Mogi had learned "SOS"—the call for help—first. Then he learned the numbers, his name, the vowels, and the rest. He remembered his troop using the code on camping trips, and the tests they gave to improve everyone's memory. He aced every test. It became so much fun that he and his dad set up a keyset in the garage and ran wires into his bedroom, where he had his own keyset. His dad was not as fast as he was, but they both enjoyed sending messages back and forth.

Mogi wrote the letters and numbers of Morse code into his notebook, plus the various protocol signals—how to cancel a letter, how to cancel a sentence, how to start over, and so on. Then, with the written code in hand, he looked at the dots and dashes in the logbook.

Nothing made sense. He could make out some series to be something, like three dashes for the letter O, but then he had a dash or a dot left over, or it was followed by a bunch of dashes, which was no letter at all. He now understood why the dispatcher's code had been ignored. With seemingly random dashes and dots, there was no chance of decoding any kind of message.

Mogi copied the logbook's string of dots and dashes into his notebook. Then he tore out both the page with the non-message and the page with his Morse code definitions. He stuffed them into his wallet, telling himself he'd work on it whenever he got a chance.

He placed the items back in the box and returned it to the closet, laying the towel over it in a certain way so that he'd recognize if someone messed with it.

CHAPTER

10

It wasn't quite nine o'clock. Mogi put his jacket on and wandered back outside. His neck and arm still hurt, and writing while leaning over a mattress had made it worse, so he hoped a short walk would relax his muscles and take away some of the pain.

As he walked past the recreation room, he looked through the window in surprise. Nancy was inside, sitting on a sofa, and next to her sat Dr. Soboknov, the Russian scientist from the museum meeting.

Pistol's words about coincidences popped into Mogi's mind as he changed direction and walked through the door.

"Mogi! You remember Dr. Soboknov, don't you?" Nancy said as the man stood and extended his hand.

"Uh, nice to see you again," Mogi said as he shook his hand.

"I called into the museum with your question about the third man. Dr. Soboknov happened to be in the museum again, so he decided to come out for a visit."

"I hope I am not intruding," the Russian man said. "I have heard about this conference center for some time, and merely used the question about the third man as an excuse to visit. It is quite a nice place. Thank you for welcoming me."

The thick accent made it difficult to understand every syllable, but he sounded sincere.

Mogi wasn't sure anymore. He couldn't ignore the fact that, after so many years of not generating any interest, a question had been asked that suddenly produced a Russian on the spot to check up on any new information. Not once, but twice.

A chill went down his spine—something was going on.

"Unfortunately, I find no indication there was a third man," Dr. Soboknov continued. "I texted a colleague back home. If there was a third man, and if he had been a Soviet agent, it would have shown up in our documents. Without a mention, any unidentified people must have been on your side and not ours."

"OK, well, thanks for looking into it," Mogi said.

Nancy continued talking with the professor, about his work, his university in Russia, the economic situation, the future of research.

"Um, I need to go," Mogi said. "Big day tomorrow. Nice to see you again." He went back to his room.

"What's up, roomie?" Pistol said, coming through the bathroom doorway as Mogi entered his room.

"The Russian guy is back, the guy from the museum. He decided to come over and visit Nancy for a while."

"There you go. I told you somebody would be watching you. The guy's a spy."

"Don't tell me he's a spy! You don't know that."

"I saw it on TV. Spies are everywhere. There are as many spies now as there were in the '50s. And you found one. Or he found you. Tell me this. You think it's a coincidence him showing up twice in one week while somebody's investigating some missing plutonium? I don't think so. That's a pretty big coincidence to me. And if you don't watch out, they're going to get you alone, and you're going to be dead meat."

Mogi decided to change the subject. "I showed Nancy the picture and pointed out the hat."

"Did she believe you?

"Nah. Doesn't seem to worry her at all." Mogi didn't tell him that Nancy wanted him to stop thinking about the mystery.

"What are you doing tomorrow?" Pistol asked.

"It's our backpacking day in the woods. That's what you did first, right?"

"Yeah. Pretty cool. Made like Daniel Boone and everything, but ol' Mr. Boone didn't have to eat freeze-dried lasagna," Pistol said, making a gagging sound. "My suggestion is to squirrel away a lot of candy bars to make it through the night."

"Overnight Backpack," the schedule said. Exploring different ecological systems, witnessing different environmental zones, a strenuous experience of wilderness living. The paragraph made it sound hard. The two days on the trail would wrap up the week for Mogi and his team. Everybody would leave on Saturday.

And that would be it. Time to leave, time to go home, time to forget all about the missing plutonium, time to forget all about Nancy's problem and return to ordinary life.

Mogi had hoped for a lot more.

CHAPTER

It was Thursday, Mountain Day.

Walking to breakfast the next morning, everyone looked across the valley toward the smoke. There wasn't much to see. Only a haze hung around the mountaintops to the east, looking more like a low cloud than smoke, making most of them sure that the fire had been put out overnight. Their backpacking trip was in the same mountain range, but far to the north. Mogi figured they'd never even smell it.

"Let me give you an update on the fire," Nancy said as she met them after breakfast. "I contacted the Forest Service about six o'clock this morning. The fire covered a lot of ground yesterday because of the wind. It's about 20 percent contained right now, and they expect it to stay east and south of where it started. The good news is that the wind is much less than it was yesterday and is definitely going to the southeast, which is away from where we'll be hiking.

"The fire itself is several miles from Guaje Lake, which is our campsite for tonight. Since we're only on the trail for one day going in and one day out, I think we're in the clear. We should have a great two days."

There were now twelve students in the group. Since the overnighter took two days, two of the four groups joined each other. The first two groups, including Pistol's, had gone on Monday and Tuesday, while Mogi's group joined Jennifer's group to make the trek Thursday and Friday.

Jennifer smiled as she came up to him. "So, you going to carry some of my stuff for me?"

"Not likely. Go pick on one of these older, good-looking boys who might be anxious to help out a weak and helpless girl like you. Over there, see that guy? He looks like he's just waiting to help you out. Don't be shy. His name is Phil."

She laughed. "Well, that might work. I could probably borrow one of those battery-driven cattle prods we saw in the barn to help him improve his attitude."

They laughed. Jennifer was well-known for not tolerating jerks.

After listening to Nancy, everyone lined up at the equipment room door. Mogi was anxious to be first in line until he saw Phil was helping to pass out the equipment. He wondered if Muck and Phil had had their little talk.

It wasn't too long before he knew the answer.

"You're a dead man," Phil said in a low voice, leaning across the table.

I'll give you dead man, you jerk, Mogi thought. How about my photograph? A sudden flush of rage made him want to punch Phil, but he held it down. A little jerk goes a long way, and Mogi was about worn out putting up with Phil.

He moved past another staff member and was given a pack, a sleeping bag, and a sleeping pad. Laid out on the equipment room floor was the team equipment: tents, cook stove, fuel, aluminum pots, water pumps with filters for drinking water, a couple of collapsible, gallon-sized water jugs, and some emergency kits. Small grocery bags had been filled with packets of food and distributed with each pack so that everyone carried the same amount.

"Everybody get a personal emergency kit?" Nancy called to them as they gathered around her. She explained each item as Phil held them up: The emergency kit contained a small first aid kit, a mirror for signaling, tablets for purifying water, a whistle, a knife, fifty feet of rope, and a fist-sized packet of what looked like foil.

"This is a highly reflective blanket, sometimes called a space blanket," Nancy said as Phil unfolded the packet of foil into a thin blanket about the size of a regular bed sheet. "If you get caught at night without a jacket, you can wrap this around you to keep your body heat in. You can also use it to reflect the sun like a mirror, for signaling an airplane or a rescue party. If you're lost in a desert, you can use it to keep the sun off or, if you're in rain, you can make a tent out of it for protection. You can also fold it in a way to collect and carry water."

Once everyone had seen it, Phil wadded the foil into a ball and shot it into a trash can. Nancy gave him a stare that clearly indicated he should have folded it so it could be used.

At the end of the line stood Muck, an open box in his hands.

"Electronics, people," he was saying with a grin. "I need your cellphones, your iPads, your iPods, your tablets, and whatever else you depend on for your happiness."

"Wait a minute," Charlotte said. "I've got to have my phone. My mom might call."

"And I take pictures with mine," Ernie protested, as others joined in.

Muck just smiled. "I appreciate your loss, but I believe that we're raising a generation of people who can't think because they're constantly plugged into something. If you had read the fine print in one of our brochures, you'd know that we don't allow any electronics on the overnight hike. We want you to see, to hear, to think, to appreciate, to wonder, to experience the full experience that Nature has to offer, not talk to somebody, or read something, or play music, or play games, or all that other stuff you're hooked on. So, lemme have 'em! I'll lock everything up tonight and you can get them back when you return tomorrow."

Mogi hated to give up his phone, and it was really going to cramp Jennifer's style. He should have read the information, he guessed, but how was he going to know what was happening in the world if he didn't have his phone? He was going to feel naked.

Moving into the parking lot, Mogi laid out his equipment on the asphalt and took inventory. It always amazed him how much stuff had to be carried for just one night out. He got to work.

Most of the teens had never carried a backpack, so he and Jennifer helped the others, sympathizing that there was so much stuff and so little pack and that the packs were heavy and awkward. At least two people had loaded their packs and then discovered they'd forgotten their portion of the food, or a big cook pot, or their water containers.

Mogi helped load the finished packs into a trailer attached to one of the center's vans and then joined the others inside the equipment room as they waited on Nancy. She was on the phone in the administration offices. Almost thirty minutes later, she returned with a ranch hand who was toting a large pack of his own.

"I'm going to have to go into town for a little business," Nancy said. "This is Hank Stevens. He's going to guide you up to tonight's campsite. The staff of the team joining us has today off, so Hank and Phil and I will be the staff people for the trip. I'll get my work done in town and will only be two or three hours behind you when I leave the trailhead. I'll catch up with you before you get to camp."

The two vans and the trailer drove out the main gate on the road toward town. A few minutes later, they turned left and crossed through another gate. It took another fifteen minutes to drive across a pasture, up around a rock outcropping, and into a parking lot at the beginning of the hiking trail.

As the students and staff unloaded the equipment, the wind whipped a gust of dust across the parking lot. They all hoisted their packs and hiked out of the parking lot onto a well-worn path that moved up and into the trees.

Everyone expected to be at Guaje Lake by supper, have a great evening, get up early the next morning for a pancake and Spam breakfast, hike back by the same trail, and be back at the parking lot by mid-afternoon. They would turn in their equipment, have a special end-of-the-week barbeque, and meet for a wrap-up of the conference.

It was 10:30 on Thursday morning.

*   *   *

Right behind the van, Nancy pulled through the preserve gate and headed to the lab. She did not like sending a group off without her. The kids were hers, she thought. She had designed the educational program, and the overnight trip was the high point. The other days were important and gave the teams good fundamentals about the environment, but leaving civilization behind and going high into the mountains? Well, special things happened there. That was when young people learned of the bond between humans and nature.

Sleeping out in the deep forest, walking through the tundra of the high country, seeing the flowers and the grasses, putting their hands into a snow-fed mountain lake, witnessing the splendor of the alpine beauty, looking at the night sky that went on forever—it brought out deep-down feelings, from the gut.

It was something very special, not only for her kids, but for herself. It reminded her of who she was.

What a rotten time for Washington to call! Some bureaucrat in the Office of Management and Budget was demanding a budget summary for her research proposals by the end of the day. So she had to hurry up and send it, just so it could sit on some guy's desk for a month.

Thirty minutes to the lab, an hour or so to get the summary done, thirty minutes to get back, fifteen minutes to the trail-head, four hours to the campsite. She'd move faster by herself, so that helped considerably.

It should be fine. Everything should be fine. Hank knew what he was doing. Everything would be fine.

She kept her foot steady on the accelerator and headed for the pass.

But when she crossed over the pass, everything was not fine.

Smoke was everywhere. It was a lot worse than anybody had said. As she took the curves faster than she should have, Nancy kept looking up, trying to see any edges of the smoke, anything that would tell her which direction the wind was blowing. She wasn't quite sure, and she hated to think so, but it looked like the wind had shifted toward the northeast.

OK, OK, she told herself. That's it. I'm calling the game. I'll get the summary sent, I'll get back, I'll radio Hank to turn everyone around, and they'll be out before the middle of the afternoon. No reason to take chances.

Muck would be watching. She smiled and relaxed a little. If there were anyone she could trust, it was Muck. He was always watching. He'd know to pull the plug.

*   *   *

Hank was a strong hiker. Twenty-five years old, he worked at the conference center during the fall and winter and as a ranch hand during the spring and summer.

The hikers had strung out along the trail. Everyone was concentrating on putting one foot in front of the other. During breaks, Hank kept the teens occupied with stories of running off coyotes, trapping and relocating bears that wandered too close to the center, and rounding up cattle after lightning storms. He laughed a lot, and that helped everyone relax.

Phil, on the other hand, had only insults for the fledgling hikers. Mogi stayed away from him by hiking last in line, and it was no surprise that Jennifer was right next to him. At every rest stop, Phil paraded up and down the line, giving "encouragement" to the hikers, which amounted to belittling their efforts and their speed. Phil would then race ahead so he'd be the first up the trail, calling for everyone to catch up with him. At every opportunity, Phil wanted to be the example to follow and the example that everyone failed to achieve.

When they stopped for lunch, Hank realized the radio was still in Nancy's backpack. It was standard procedure to make a radio call every four hours or so, to check in for weather advisories, report broken equipment, request help for sick or injured people, etc.

"Nancy will be here before anything exciting happens, so we'll keep going up," he told the group. "Everybody OK?"

Everybody said yes, but it wasn't true. Sharon, the girl from Green River, was not feeling well. Jennifer saw it first. Walking behind her, she knew the girl was having trouble breathing. And her head must have been hurting because she had chugged a couple of aspirin and then four more an hour later.

Finishing a break, the group re-shouldered their packs and headed up the trail. Mogi looked up at the ridges above them. He could see the tall pines swaying back and forth, their branches moving up and down. The wind must be pretty strong up there, he thought. Good thing it's still blowing east.

But it wasn't blowing east. The trail had wound through a valley and up into a canyon, making a fishhook-shaped loop before it crested the ridge. Mogi hadn't noticed he was turned around.

The wind was blowing—blowing hard—to the north.

Straight toward them.

CHAPTER
12

The announcement came at eleven o'clock.
The lab was closing immediately. Everybody go home, immediately.

Nancy's heart was in her throat, and her stomach churned. She had given an honest effort to get the summary done. Now she didn't care. Washington be hanged.

She tried again to call the conference center from her office phone. No one answered. She tried again. Then with her cellphone. Nothing.

She knew the communication lines into the mountains ran south of the road, closer to where the fire had been burning yesterday, so the hard lines between the lab and the ranch could be damaged. If they were burned, the fire might have gotten the cellphone tower as well. That's why the cellphone wasn't working.

Racing to the Suburban to get back to the ranch, she almost got out and strangled the state policeman blocking the road into the mountains.

Closed. Closed. Closed.

No one was going anywhere on that road.

She tried to explain, and she knew the officer was being more than reasonable, but the fire had shot across a narrow place in the road and was now burning on both sides of the asphalt not far ahead. They would not let anybody drive through a forest fire.

The wind was strong enough to rock her car as she turned around and pulled off the road. What now? The fire was still miles away from the kids. Muck would know what was going on. He'd probably already gotten them turned around and headed back home.

She calculated the time it would take to circle around the mountains and come into the conference center from the west. One hour to get from Los Alamos to Santa Fe, another thirty minutes directly south almost to Albuquerque, maybe another hour west and north to get to Jemez Springs, and another thirty back to the preserve.

She took off, dodging the fire trucks that were massing on the road.

It was 11:30 on Thursday morning.

"Suck it up, you people. We don't tolerate wimps in this outfit," Phil called over his shoulder.

Mogi and Jennifer were both watching Sharon. She was strong—they had to give her that. It wasn't until they had followed a trail that circled around the top of a canyon and crossed over a ridge that she finally threw up. It wasn't mild, either. After falling down onto her hands and knees and wretching up everything, she finally rolled over on her back.

"You don't look so good," Hank said as he got her to sit up and swallow some water.

"My head is killing me!" she said and then starting crying.

"You dizzy?"

"Yeah."

"Your head hurts pretty bad?"

"Oh, yeah. It feels like somebody's swinging a sledge hammer inside."

"Have you had any shakes or trembling?"

"Just before I threw, up but I don't think so now."

Hank helped her to lie back down. "Everybody gather around," he called to the others.

"Sharon has altitude sickness. That's not unusual or especially bad, and if we had an extra day, she could ride it out, but our practice is to take people with altitude sickness back to the center. Going down in altitude is the only thing you can do. The problem is that I went off and forgot the radio, so I can't call for someone to come and help her get down.

"That means that all of you need to wait here until I get back. Hopefully, I'll meet Nancy on the way down."

"Don't worry about us," Phil said. "I know where we're going and we'll make it there in plenty of time."

"I don't want you to go on. You need to stay here until Nancy comes," Hank told him.

"What do you mean? We don't need Nancy. I mean, she can catch up to us, no problem."

Hank took Phil by the arm and led him away from the group. Mogi watched as they argued for several minutes. He could see that Hank finally just told Phil what to do. As he walked back to the group, Phil's eyes burned with anger.

"OK. I'm going to take Sharon back. I bet I won't get much past the ridge before I meet Nancy. I'm surprised she hasn't caught us already. She'll come on to meet you, while I go out with Sharon." Hank went through Sharon's backpack, taking out whatever food and equipment would be needed by the others, and gave it to Phil. Then he strapped her pack onto his.

"What I need from all of you is to sit tight. Phil will be in charge, but you are to stay here. Nancy will adjust the schedule when she joins you. Get yourselves some snacks, and don't start any fires or light any stoves. You guys stay together. Nobody wanders off. OK?"

That seemed fine to everyone. They moved off the trail, dropped their packs, and plopped down on the ground. The plastic sacks that held food came out immediately, with the hikers descending like vultures on the snacks.

"I think I'm dying," Henry said as he spread out over a bed of pine needles.

"You smell like you already did," Charlotte quipped.

Sharon struggled to her feet, took a deep breath, and started slowly walking down the trail. Three minutes and they were out of sight.

"All right, children," Phil said with a sarcastic tone, "don't wander off." He walked up the trail and disappeared.

It was 3:00 on Thursday afternoon.

Jim Daniels called it an explosion.

The weather front coming from the north continued to slide south into Arizona, crowding the other front to the east and making the channel of high-speed air change its direction. The channel was bent northward, causing it to stream up the western edge of the Rio Grande valley and to track up against the sides of the mountains above Los Alamos.

With the air acting like a bellows, with new fuel and a clear path to the high country, the fire exploded north like a freight train, leaping over the highway and rushing headlong into the undergrowth-rich forest on the eastern flank of the Jemez, gobbling up hundred-foot timbers with two-hundred-foot flames in a matter of minutes.

In only a matter of hours, the leading edge of the fire had completely changed directions: skirting the laboratory property and racing up the mountains next to the city. It was headed to a tall ridge on the south side of the deep canyon that separated LANL property from the town of Los Alamos.

Jim traced the outline of the ridge on the map with a black marker. The canyon was deep and it was wide, maybe wide enough that the embers would be blown into the canyon and not across. There was a road at the bottom of the canyon, allowing water trucks to reach any small fires. Air tankers could also coat the sides of the canyon to prevent blazes going up.

That ridge was the battleground. The war would be lost or won along that ridge. If embers or sparks got across the canyon, they'd land in yards and on the tops of houses.

He ordered all bulldozers to the ridge. He needed a lane of clear dirt, four bulldozers wide. A lane big enough to hold that fire. All the hotshots were to follow the bulldozers, cutting the fallen timbers and cleaning the brush out of the path of the fire. Directly across the other side of the canyon, city firefighters were wetting down areas along the streets.

The county police began evacuating homes directly across from the ridge. To the residents rushing out of their homes, it was a nightmare come to life, a shock of reality compared with what just days before had been unimaginable.

By four o'clock in the afternoon, more than five hundred firefighters were working feverishly, facing a fire far bigger and more ferocious than most had ever seen.

The fire bombers had helped for a while, but when the winds gusted over sixty miles an hour, they were grounded. It was the same with the three firefighting helicopters; even the spotter planes weren't allowed up.

By mid-afternoon, the cloud of smoke, ten times its size since early that morning, shrouded the forest, the town, and the lab in darkness.

* * *

The wheels of the Suburban skidded as they moved off the highway onto the pavement of the preserve road. Nancy turned the wheel too tightly, and the backend was thrown to the right, barely missing the gate. She kept her foot down until she could see a van parked next to the main building.

Thank God! They were already back.

Her pulse rate immediately slowed, and she felt relief flow through her body. She pulled into a spot, got out, and went to the equipment room. Her group would either be there or in the cafeteria, or maybe the common room. As she rounded the corner, she saw Muck walking toward her.

"Darlin', I am so happy to see you," Muck said as he grinned. "I bet you and your kids have had quite an adventure."

Nancy's stomach twisted again. She realized that the van parked next to the building didn't have a trailer attached.

"I wasn't with the kids—I had to go into town. Hank's with the kids. They're not here?"

Muck's face turned grim. "I haven't seen Hank. I've been in the north pasture since before you left this morning. You haven't heard from him?"

Nancy turned and started running for the Suburban. Muck caught up with her and led her to the equipment room.

"Let's try the radio," he said as he crossed to a shelf full of electronics.

"You mean he didn't call in? He should have—" she caught herself in mid-sentence. "Oh, no! The radio is still in my pack!" She looked at Muck with an expression of shock and horror. "What have I done?"

Muck moved to the wall and picked up a phone. His mind was moving through a checklist. He called the main house and told them of the possible emergency: There's a group of a dozen out on the Guaje trail, possibly at high camp, maybe in path of the fire. He needed a report from the Forest Service on the fire; he needed Jim Daniels to know there'd be a possible rescue operation; and he'd be on the radio in the next few minutes.

He grabbed a radio off a charger on the shelf and made for the door, Nancy close behind.

Did Hank turn around? Are the kids already out? If not, how far did they go in, and where are they now? Where's the fire? Is the trail clear?

They talked as fast as Muck drove. Coming up a rise before the turnoff to the trailhead, they could see the smoke was halfway down the mountains. It was a deep, black smoke where there had been no smoke at all that morning. The wind whipped against their vehicle as they watched trees on a distant mountain rim flail against each other.

The sky had darkened, and the air was filled with ash as they pulled into the trailhead parking lot. When Nancy saw the two figures sitting wearily on the side of the trail, her heart fell. She jumped out the door before the vehicle came to a stop.

"Hank! Hank! Where are the kids? Look at me, where are the kids?"

Hank was having trouble breathing, his face covered with sweat and blackened with soot and ash. He took a moment to focus as Nancy bent over him.

Muck moved to Sharon, laying her fully on the ground, examining her, mentally going through his EMT checklist. Though weak, she seemed OK. Her headache had gone away as soon as they got to the parking lot, but now she was hacking and coughing, her chest shuddering, her face wearied with pain. After leaving the group above, Sharon and Hank had slowly made their way to the ridge. From there, they could see the heavy smoke column in the distance. The smoke was still going upward at the time, so Hank wasn't concerned. It was just smoke. Sharon had folded over and thrown up again, so he helped her to her feet and they moved along as fast as they could. There was no alternative—she had to get out.

He kept looking down the trail, hoping for Nancy to appear.

They wound around the fishhook and hit the falling ash. It had been trapped on the western face of the mountains and was flowing into any canyon that opened to the sky. After that, it became difficult to breathe, the smoke thick and putrid and filled with chunks of flying embers, burning bark, and smoldering pine needles. He could see no flames, and the smoke was swirling, not blasting up as if there were a fire below.

It was hot—stifling hot—dark, and hard to see. It was hard to walk as the two moved down the trail, but Hank didn't dare turn back. Wrapping T-shirts across their faces and leaving Sharon's pack behind, they stumbled forward as fast as they could, running when the path was clear.

Muck helped Sharon into the back seat of the Suburban. Nancy steadied Hank as he crawled in the other side. Muck and Nancy exchanged glances as they turned the big vehicle around and sped toward the road.

Muck had forced himself to not go up the trail. He knew better. If there was smoke when Hank was there, now there was fire. And at least the kids had Phil to guide them; he knew the trails.

That way is no longer open, he thought to himself. We've got to find another way to get to those kids.

It was 5:00 on Thursday afternoon.

* * *

An hour later, in the premature darkness of a sun blotted out by smoke, Mogi Franklin was one of eleven scared teenagers huddled on a narrow trail high in the mountains.

"Something's wrong, really wrong. I mean, Nancy should be here by now."

"Where's Phil? Isn't he supposed to be taking care of us?"

"We're doing what we've been told. We need to stay where we are!"

"I bet he's up there somewhere, watching us and laughing."

"How are we going to know if she's not coming? What if something happened and nobody's coming?"

"Do you think Hank will be coming back? If he didn't find Nancy, will he leave Sharon with the van and come back for us?"

"Can we eat this stuff cold? I'm starving."

Everyone was talking at once. Even Mogi couldn't stop his mouth. The teens would stand up, rant, walk back and forth, and then collapse into a sitting position, all the while trying to find a solution to their predicament.

"What are we going to do? We can't just sit here!" Charlotte cried out.

"Let's go back to the ridge," someone said.

"It makes sense," another agreed.

"Without packs, we could make it pretty quick," a third observed.

"It would give us a good view of what's happening."

"Maybe we'll see Nancy coming up the trail, or even meet Hank on his way back."

It was agreed.

Full of anxious energy, each burst from their sitting places and ran—fast, as if they couldn't help it. Only Jennifer was left. She did not run off with the others, taking time instead to rummage through the pile of food sacks, and then followed. When the crowd reached the ridge, everyone was sucking wind pretty bad.

But they got what they came for.

The sun was low on the horizon, far in the west, so it lit the forest and hills under the smoke. It was hard to figure out the shape of the billowing smoke, but the huge cloud seemed as if it were going up and to the left. Mogi looked around and thought about where the center was, what the mountains around it looked like, which direction the sun was.

East. The smoke is going east. He breathed more slowly. That's good. It's not coming toward us.

There was no sign of Hank, or Nancy, so, buffeted by the wind, the group forced themselves to go back, disappointed that they had found no remedy to their problem.

Phil was at the trail when they got back. He was sitting on a rock, not seeming at all bothered by the circumstances. "I was afraid you wimps chickened out and went back home."

No one wanted to say anything, but John finally spoke. "We went up to see how the fire looked."

"So, you think the fire's OK? You're ready for supper? Ready for beddy-bye?"

"Where's the food?" Mogi asked. He had just noticed— all of the food sacks had disappeared. The hikers gathered in front of Phil.

"The dweeb wants to know where the food is. Well, gee, I thought you guys wanted to experience the backcountry. Be tough. Be strong. I thought you'd appreciate a more challenging experience."

"Oh, I'm sorry. Are we talking about food? You guys want a snack?" Jennifer held up the plastic sack she had been carrying.

Phil was surprised, grew red in the face, and then jumped at her to grab the sack. She pulled it away from him as Mogi moved between them. Mogi planted his foot on the trail and casually bumped Phil's hip enough that he went sprawling into the dirt. Furious, Phil scrambled to his feet and shoved his face within a couple of inches of Mogi's nose.

Mogi did not flinch. Phil started shaking.

"Lookie here," Phil said between his gritted teeth. "The mystery man steps forward. What's the matter, mystery man? You want to fix ol' Nancy's problem for her? You want to clear her old man, but you can't figure it out, can you? Want to know what happened to the plane?"

Phil moved his face even closer to Mogi's.

"You can't figure it out, can you? Feeling stupid? Maybe because you are stupid, dweeb. You can't figure out that they took the plane apart and put it in a truck, can you?"

Mogi's expression did not change. This was not the time. This was about a group of backpackers in danger.

But for a split-second, in just a glimpse of a thought, he couldn't help but think about it. Took the plane apart. Of course, dork-boy. It landed, they took off the wings, and they pushed it all into the back of an eighteen-wheeler. They could have been in Arizona by breakfast and no one would have ever seen the plane again.

It was bad enough to not have thought of that, but to be trumped by this jerk made it worse.

"What do you want, Phil?" Mogi asked in an even voice. Phil hesitated when Mogi did not move.

"Want? I only want to provide you with a rich experience in leadership," he said with a laugh. "But maybe not the way Mr. Jones wants. Maybe Muck doesn't understand what real leadership is because he's too soft."

Mogi felt heat rising behind his eyes.

"I believe that you Boy Scouts don't appreciate me. I think you need to learn a lesson." Phil turned and picked up his pack, shouldered it, and moved up the trail. "Don't get lost."

"Hey, you can't leave us!"

"You're going to get in trouble for this!"

"Go on, leave, you jerk! We don't need you."

"You're going to get fired for this!"

Phil never looked back and soon was lost in the trees ahead of them. The group steamed and stewed for a while longer, but eventually grew quiet. They were alone and afraid. Jennifer handed out candy bars, fruit cups, and trail mix packets, the snacks quickly grabbed by people whose hunger was being overwhelmed by a sense of desperation and fear.

"How'd you know he was going to steal the food?" Mogi asked her later.

She gave him a grim smile. "Bullies are always easy to figure out."

It was 6:30 on Thursday evening.

CHAPTER

BREAKING NEWS FROM CHANNEL 14 NEWS: LOS ALAMOS ON FIRE!

STUDIO: Jeremy Edwards

"Good evening. I'm Jeremy Edwards, with Action 14 News.

"It is now eight o'clock. For those of you just joining us, let us repeat the information we just received from Jim Daniels, the incident commander of what has been officially named the 'Mesa Grande' fire. From a planned controlled burn four days ago to a fire-ravaged countryside today, we've been with you. But it now seems that the worst may still be yet to come.

"We go now to Michael Tumbah, who is on the scene in Los Alamos. Michael, can you tell us the latest information?"

REMOTE: Michael Tumbah

"Jeremy, we knew it was bad, but a new development makes it a whole new ballgame. There is a group of teen-age backpackers somewhere in the mountains west of Los Alamos. With all this destruction going on around us, with the forest going up in flames before our eyes, we have at least been consoled by the fact that not one life has been lost. More than six hundred firefighters and support people, on the ground and in the air, have fought this fire without injury. This may now be coming to an end.

"The Valles Caldera National Preserve Conference Center has told us that a group of teen-agers on a research trip in the Jemez Mountains may now be directly in the path of this fire. Jim Daniels, the Forest Service official in charge of fighting this fire, was notified this afternoon by the conference center that a group of fourteen backpackers went into the mountains this morning, thinking at the time that they would be safe from the fire and would be in and out by tomorrow with no problem.

"Two of the group returned because of altitude sickness, but the rest kept going. Early this morning, their expected route was not in danger from the fire, but with the wind dramatically shifting and increasing this afternoon, the path of the firestorm is now directly in line with the group's position. I'm keeping my ears open for any new developments and will bring any news immediately as soon as we know more.

"As an update, the fire is holding. Since early this afternoon, a dozen bulldozers have been working high on the south ridge of Los Alamos Canyon. In an effort to keep the fire on the south side of the canyon, this fire line is the extraordinary work of the bulldozer operators and hundreds of firefighters working together. If the fire line continues to hold, the homes on the other side of Los Alamos Canyon, directly across from the flames on the south ridge of the canyon, will be safe. More than thirty cities and counties in New Mexico, Arizona, and Colorado have sent firefighting units to the area, and many of them are now working the streets in the city, across from the south ridge where the fire is currently burning, doing what they can to prepare for the worst.

"But the winds keep coming, Jeremy. I have never, ever, in all my years of living in New Mexico, seen winds this strong. You can see from my jacket and from the trees behind me—there's a shot of the trees behind me—that the wind is just ferocious. It is hard for me to even stand upright. They have grounded all slurry bombers, all helicopters, all scout planes. Even SkyCam has been ordered to stay on the ground at the airport. Nothing can fly in this wind without somebody risking life and limb.

"That's about the way it is here, Jeremy. We're staying here, in the middle of the action. This is Michael Tumbah, Channel Fourteen News, reporting from the county building in Los Alamos."

STUDIO: Jeremy Edwards

"Thank you, Michael. We are all praying that the fire line holds. Now for other news. . . ."

* * *

It was 8:05 on Thursday evening.

Nancy stared at her coffee cup while Muck looked at a map that was spread out on the equipment room's table. The topographic map included the Guaje Lake area, clearly showing the trails, peaks, wooded areas, meadows, canyons, cliffs, and a patch of blue for the lake. They knew exactly where the kids had been left by Hank—a small dot Muck had placed with his pen.

They were halfway to the lake, only a couple of ridges away, with two hard climbs and then a steep slope down into Guaje Canyon; maybe a couple of miles, but it was all above 10,000 feet, making the going tough. The hike from the trailhead was hard but do-able in a day, giving the kids a challenging but rewarding experience when they reached the lake, one of the prettiest spots in Northern New Mexico. Mountain Day was always the favorite activity of the conference attendees.

South of his small dot, four and a half miles from the lake, Muck had drawn lines and figures showing the fire's position, from information given to him by the Forest Service people working with Jim Daniels—where the current fire line was, where the bulldozers were working, where the crews had been assigned, where they had been earlier, the strategy of how they were working the fire.

Muck was well-known to the local Forest Service. Even though they resented the lectures he boldly gave them during public meetings, they knew he spoke with in-the-trenches experience. He had been a smokejumper commander, a hardened warrior who had fought fires across the western states, Canada, and Alaska.

So they gave him whatever he asked for. Especially since these were ranch kids. That made them Muck's kids.

They also knew Nancy and had a much better relationship with her. She had worked for the Forest Service and then had acted as a consultant for a number of years, helping to initiate lab programs that provided funds that benefited both the lab and the forest agencies.

So they gave her whatever she asked for. These kids were Nancy's kids.

The fire had moved into the Guaje Trail area below the fishhook, cutting off any path for fire crews to go in from the trailhead parking lot. But, on the east side of the mountains, the fire line to the south of Los Alamos Canyon was holding, giving the backpackers time to keep going north, all the way to the lake. That was the current best bet. The backpackers would make it to the lake and the fire would burn itself out on the ridge, miles from their camp. They'd be dirty, scared out of their minds, and tired. They'd have trouble breathing after inhaling soot and smoke for a day or two, but they'd be alive.

Wait until morning. Forest fires always calm down overnight because of the lower temperature and higher humidity. In the morning, we'll get them home. We'll do something and we'll get them home. That was Jim Daniels' promise.

Muck wasn't so sure. He'd worked with fire agencies for many years, and the agencies were more conservative now than ever. No one liked to put their firefighters in danger, but the government had new rules, new measures of safety, new procedures that stressed caution, new regulations that made discussion more important than action. The big thing of the day was "risk management," and organizations were instructed to have multiple layers of approval so "better" decisions could be made. It all added up, Muck thought, to throwing decision-makers like Jim Daniels into battles with one hand tied behind his back.

Nancy kept staring at her coffee cup, wishing a millionth time for a do-over.

"I was on a fire up in Wyoming once," Muck said as he leaned back in his chair. "It was a big summer for lightning, and we had been chasing little fires every day and night for a month. But this one was one to remember.

"Lightning hit a tree on the side of a hill, right in the middle of a grove of aspens. It had been a dry spring, and the forest was like a tinderbox. On the day the lightning hit, you had to spit twice to get any water to the ground. Anyway, it was one tree on fire for about two minutes, then two, then ten, and within an hour, the whole hillside in flames.

"Well, the hillside was the lower part of an enclosed valley. At the top of the valley was a Boy Scout camp, with several buildings, all wood, all surrounded by thick forest. Before the camp even knew there was a fire in the canyon below them, the fire jumped across to the other hillside." He drew imaginary lines on the table. "Just like that, the only way to get out of the valley was closed off."

"Was anybody there?"

"Oh, yeah. Forty-two teen-agers and seven adults."

"What did they do?"

"Well, the fire naturally burned upward, toward the camp. Since there were people involved, I was sent in with my crew. They couldn't get helicopters into the valley because the winds generated by the fire were awful, so they dropped us onto a ridge and we walked down to the camp.

"The first thing we did was set some fires."

Nancy gave a little laugh. "Oh, hey, that's smart. You set backfires?"

Muck grinned. "In the center of the camp was a big pasture of dry grass where they played baseball, so we set it on fire in as many places as we could. The grass burned like straw and everything was black in about twenty minutes.

"They had this big bus, a regular school bus-type bus, right? We got everybody out in the center of the pasture with whatever they could find—shovels, rakes, hoes—and knocked down what was now just embers and ash so that, if the fire made it to the pasture, it wouldn't have anything to burn because we had already burned it."

"I bet the scouts thought you were crazy."

"I drove the bus and parked it smack dab in the middle of the burnt grass. The camp had a big water tank that ran off a well, so we got everybody scurrying all over the place to get the water hoses that were used to water the grass, gardens, and trees. We hooked the hoses end to end and stretched them all the way out to that bus. We put the sprinklers around it and on top of it, turned them on, and, when we saw the flames charging up the road, everybody got inside the bus."

Muck started laughing.

"It was crazy inside that bus! We had the scouts and the adults and then ten of us jumpers, and everybody's talking or screaming or crying or laughing, and then, here comes the fire. We see the flames close in on the front gate, then it's going up both sides of the camp, and pretty soon one of the buildings is burning, and then another, and more people are screaming, and it's absolutely nuts in that bus. Man, we were feeling like pieces of chicken in a barbeque grill!

"However, what we had planned was working. The fire stayed away from the bus, the sprinklers kept spraying water because we had been smart enough to put sprinklers on the hoses themselves and on the water tower to keep them all from melting. We thought we were doing pretty good.

"Of course, we've got the water spraying all over the bus to keep us from burning, and it's hotter than blazes, so everybody in the bus is sweating like crazy. We had made a gigantic sauna. So, pretty soon, everybody's taking off their clothes, right down to their underwear!" Muck started waving his arms like he was trying to cool off.

"And then the water runs out!"

Nancy was shaking her head and laughing as Muck grew more animated.

"We're sweating like crazy, and we're gagging at the smell, and it's getting hotter and hotter, and we're looking pretty naked, if I do say so myself. So, I said to myself, we've used up that trick, what else can we do? I knew we could stay in the bus and not burn by fire, but I wasn't sure that we wouldn't melt or at least roast to a medium well. I'd been using the radio, telling them what we were doing, and then it went dead.

"I was wondering if we should make a mad dash for it when, suddenly, from up in the sky, we hear this low-level run by a tanker. He drops a load of retardant directly in front of us in the direction of the road. Right behind him we hear another tanker going in the same direction but farther down, dumping their loads right on the road, so we figured that they were trying to tell us something.

"I jumped into the driver's seat, started the engine, and down the road we went, out of the camp, through the canyon, through the fire, and out the other side. We were flying! By the time we made it out, the tires were smoking so bad we looked like a comet!"

"So everybody made it OK?" Nancy asked.

"Everybody made it OK." Muck grinned. "It was quite an adventure. The camp was toast, but nobody was hurt."

Nancy turned back to her coffee. Muck returned to his map for a moment and then spoke again.

"The truth is, I have never been as up-against-the-wall as that moment. I was the leader, and I didn't know what to do. My team was full of leaders, and they didn't know what to do. And everybody else had lost their minds, so they weren't any help.

"But we forced ourselves to be ready, to be ready to do whatever it took. And when we saw those bombers plowing a way for us, we never hesitated. Thank goodness there was someone, somewhere, who was thinking of what we would be thinking, so that they ordered those bombers to make us a way out.

"I hope those kids are paying attention. They need to be ready, but I can't guess for what."

It was 9:00 on Thursday night.

*   *   *

At 1:30 in the darkness of the early morning hours on Friday, the sirens blew. The fire department didn't even know if they would work because they'd stopped testing them in the mid-'70s. Civil Defense or Air Raid or whatever you wanted to call them, the sirens blew.

Evacuate! Fire! Fire! Fire! Evacuate!

The county police, augmented by the state police and the protection force from the laboratory, blared out warnings in the western areas first and then throughout the town.

The battle on the ridge had been lost.

The winds had not quieted down as expected. Gusts of 45 to 55 MPH had rolled burning logs and branches across the fire line into the unburned forest of the canyon below, creating huge tornado-like swirls of embers and ashes, drawing them high above the ground and shooting them back to earth like a burning exhaust, scattering them over the far canyon walls and onto the houses beyond.

From on top of a building downtown, the long-range lens of a network TV camera caught a brief glimpse of a flare-up. Adjusting the focus quickly, the reporter zeroed in on the image: A straight line of flame along a roof, the latticework of a window, the explosion of a propane bottle from a barbecue grill.

Los Alamos was on fire.

It was 1:31 on Friday morning.

*   *   *

Before even the slightest hint of dawn, the phone rang next to Muck's bed. The call, from the Central Fire Management Headquarters in Grand Junction, Colorado, did not wake him because he wasn't asleep. He took the news quietly, thanked his friend for the call, hung up, and slipped into his clothes.

He went down the hallway and found Nancy sitting on the side of her bed. She had heard the phone ring. She did not need to ask what it was about. While she dressed, Muck went to the equipment building.

Muck raised the big door, went to his office, and unlocked the steel mesh door. He pulled a monstrous bag from the shelves and set it on the equipment room floor. Another big bag followed. He pulled a few more bags down, unhooked one of the overstuffed body suits from its hanger, threw it on top of the bags, and set a large helmet on the desk.

He slipped on the yellow shirt.

Nancy joined him. Together, they carried the equipment into the dining hall. Muck started emptying the bags as Nancy moved the folding tables end-to-end to make one long table.

A table long enough to lay out a parachute.

He was crazy.

She was crazy.

But those kids were *their* kids, and they didn't need a committee to tell them to risk everything.

*   *   *

Mogi lay on his sleeping bag, but there wasn't a chance he was going to sleep. The air above him was smoky. He had seen stars in the north sky hours earlier, but there was nothing but darkness now.

It's not that bad, he kept thinking. If it were that bad, they would have come after us, and nothing would have stopped them. They would have sent a helicopter, if nothing else. So everything's cool.

Having all privately decided to pretend they were sleeping, each of the eleven teens had found a spot on the trail and rolled out his or her bag and pad.

Mogi could hear someone crying. He wasn't sure who it was, but it could have been anyone. They were all still waiting for Nancy to come down the trail. They'd tell her everything and they'd get out of there and Phil would never work for the conference center again and it would serve him right and they'd all go back home.

Where was she? Why wasn't she here?

Mogi had told the others it wasn't that bad, but he was thinking that maybe it was. Something had gone wrong. Maybe he'd wander back up to the ridge and see if anything had changed.

He hadn't gone a dozen steps before Jennifer appeared next to him. She was shaking.

Hiking up wasn't as hard as before, since they weren't running, but the trail appeared entirely different—it was covered in gray and white ash. A few minutes later, holding their flashlight beams out in front, the trail disappeared into a cloud of smoke—not a steady cloud, but a billowing torrent of smoke just as the trail topped the ridge.

Moving up to the ridge, staying low as the smoke surrounded him and covering his mouth with his T-shirt, Mogi bent low, shielded his eyes, and struggled the last few feet. Jennifer did the same, but had taken hold of Mogi's hand.

They hunkered down as the wind hit them. It was three times as fierce on the ridge as it was just twenty steps down the trail.

Mogi glanced across the canyon. Through the swirling haze, he could see that someone had set up lights on the ridge. Big lanterns or something.

His heart sank as he understood what he was looking at: flames. Huge flames. Monstrous flames. Whole trees lit up like matchsticks, with swirls of flame shooting above them and curling into strange shapes before the trees vanished into a pure yellow light. He tried to remember, tried to get his bearings. The burning trees were higher up, another ridge over, maybe two, from where they stood.

Another gust swirled the smoke around them. Mogi's eyes immediately closed to the stinging wind, and he lost his balance and fell. Jennifer's hand was lost in the smoke.

He thought he heard her screaming. Huddling in the dirt as the wind whipped ash all around him, choking on the smoke and ash and embers as they singed his skin, he could do nothing but cover his face and turn his back against the forces pushing him. He scooted in the direction of the trail and dragged himself downward until he was below the smoke.

His mind flashed on an image of one of the posters at the museum, a blowup of London during the war. Skeletons of buildings rising up out of mounds of brick and cement while huge flames shot out of the structures behind. When the bombs fell.

This must have been what it was like when the bombs fell.

That's when he figured out that it wasn't Jennifer who was screaming, but himself. He was screaming and stumbling and blind.

A hand grabbed him and held him.

"Listen to me!" Jennifer screamed at him. "Look at me! Look at me! Let me see your eyes!"

He was in her grip. He looked into her eyes in the dim flashlight beam.

"Now is not the time to lose it! We've got things to do. Understand?"

He buried his face in her shoulder.

"Look at me!" she shouted again.

He straightened up, sniffled, took a deep breath, and exhaled.

"I need you," Jennifer said, "and you need me. All of those people down there need both of us. We've got things to do, OK?"

Mogi took another deep breath. He nodded. Jennifer let go of him and they sprinted down the trail as fast as they could go.

It was 3:00 in the blackness of Friday morning.

CHAPTER

"**Get up! Everybody get up! We've got to get out of** here! Hurry!"

Whether they had expected it or not, there was a collective sigh of relief as the teen-agers jumped to their feet. But when Mogi and Jennifer told them what they had seen, it took only a second for panic to take over.

"Listen. LISTEN!" Mogi shouted. "Forget the tents, forget the sleeping bags, forget the packs. What you need is your flashlight, your survival pack, and your water bottles. We've got to get to the lake. Keep a jacket or a sweatshirt or something, but leave everything else. NOW!"

They were on the trail in less than a minute. Jennifer stood to the side as they hustled by, making sure no one was left behind. Mogi tried to remember the map he had seen back in the center, but it was impossible. He couldn't focus, couldn't slow his breathing enough to think straight. All he wanted to do was run. Like everybody else.

They all ran, the beams of their flashlights bouncing helter-skelter across the trail, the trees, the smoke above them, on each other. In a few minutes, they heaved to the side of the trail, the ones behind piling into the ones in front, gasping for air like panicked locomotives.

"We can't keep this up," Mogi gasped. "We need to slow down."

"Does anyone remember the trail between here and the lake?" Jennifer asked.

"I don't remember. I never saw a map," one answered.

"It was supposed to be straight north, I think," another offered.

Mogi finally threw up his hands.

"OK. Let's assume that if we stay on this trail, we'll get to the lake. The fire is behind us, but we don't know how far, and the lake is in front of us, but we don't know how far. But it's far enough that we'll never make it running. Let's walk, but quickly. Watch your feet. Keep your flashlights on the trail. Watch out for each other—we can't leave anybody behind."

The line of hikers soon stretched out, Mogi and Jennifer coming last. Using all of his concentration, he kept his light on the trail in front of him, kept his breathing steady, and focused on Jennifer's footsteps.

After about a hundred feet, the others moved to the side and let Jennifer take the lead. She was a strong hiker and set a consistent pace that everyone could follow. Mogi stayed in the back.

It was 3:30 on Friday morning.

*　　*　　*

"You know you're crazy to do this," Nancy said as the Suburban barreled down the highway to the west, toward Jemez Springs and away from the conference center.

"Well, view it as a calculated risk," Muck said. "The Forest Service can't do anything that puts a rescue team in danger. The Bureau of Land Management can't do anything because the Forest Service has jurisdiction. The Department of Energy can't do anything because it'll take three days to fill out the paperwork and a month to get approval. The Los Alamos Police and Fire Departments can't do anything because they don't have the resources. Anybody else who might be a player is already busy on the fire. That leaves us.

"We know where they were and we think we know where they'll be. They're not dumb and probably didn't stay put half as long as we think they did.

"So, we guess," Muck said with an authoritative voice. "We guess that they followed the trail north, away from the fire. They're headed for the lake, because that's where the trail goes. The problem is that, if they're smart, they'll get to the lake, discover this big sign that points to the west that says 'Valles Grande,' which will translate to the conference center, and then they'll dash up the Guaje Canyon Trail west, up and out of the canyon.

"What they need is someone to tell them *not* to go west from the lake, but to stay at the lake when they get there. They don't know that the trail out of the canyon is more difficult than what they're on, and that it will take more time to get out than they think. That's why we always have our kids take the same trail out as they did hiking in. Hopefully, the fire won't reach that canyon. It's nothing but a funnel and would burn faster than anyone could make it up that trail.

"So, it's up to me and you, and I hope you remember how to fly."

Nancy gave a nervous laugh. "I remember how to fly. If my friend's plane is at his private strip on the other side of La Cueva, then we'll be in the air in about an hour. I just hope you remember how to jump."

"Oh, I remember how to jump," he said with a smile. "Let's hope I remember how to land."

It was 4:30 on Friday morning.

*   *   *

Jim Daniels was on what seemed like his twentieth cup of coffee. He watched out his window as truckloads of firefighters came off various parts of the fire, haggard and exhausted, some of them having been on the fire line for eighteen or twenty hours. Other people straggled in and out, trucks came and went with supplies, and volunteers from the Red Cross continuously dished out food from two food lines.

The firefighter camp looked like a war zone, and it wasn't clear who was winning.

It had taken nearly an hour to relay location details from Muck Jones through the Grand Junction office to the Los Alamos Command Center and then discuss the options with his team leaders, and it took twice as long to assemble two fully-equipped rescue teams and get them on the road. Two rescue teams put together in a hurry, sent into an almost totally unknown situation, and sent out in the middle of the night. He threw his coffee cup into a sink. It was too dangerous! Cutting it too thin!

Somebody's going to get hurt.

The Blue Team was going in from the east. Driving the back roads up to the entrance of Cemetery Canyon, they'd hike to the west up to Guaje Ridge. They'd work their way up the ridge and drop into Trinidad Canyon. They would need to do some bushwhacking to the trail, but it would take them right to the spot where the preserve guy said he'd left them when he'd had to get the sick girl to lower altitude. If those kids had followed orders, that's where they would be.

The Yellow Team had it easier, but it would take longer. They were driving the long way around and would make it to Los Posos Canyon from the west. There was a trailhead there with a parking lot, all located in a large meadow in the northern part of the preserve. It was close enough to the conference center to see the lights. They'd go up the trail, across the ridge, connect to the Guaje Canyon Trail, hike down into Guaje Canyon until they found the lake, and then go south on the Guaje Lake Trail. It was safer, but it was going to take two good hours just to get to the trailhead.

Two hours that those kids might not have.

The Blue Team could be to their spot sooner, but the route was more dangerous. If the fire shot north of the city before dawn, it would get into Trinidad Canyon before the team made the crossover, and the fire would be directly above them. Or the fire might drop down and get into the canyon directly below them. Jim didn't want to think about how bad it could be if the team got caught in between.

It didn't feel any better that he had given the team absolute orders to turn around if they had to. Nobody is a hero, he told them. Nobody next to you dies. Stay on the radio. Always be prepared to reverse and get out. Keep your back open.

It didn't make him feel any better at all. He knew that those men weren't going to stop if there were any chance at all of getting to those kids.

He wanted to send a chopper into Guaje Canyon, but he couldn't order a chopper into smoke in the middle of a mountain range, in the middle of the night, in the middle of hurricane winds, no matter how much he wanted to. If the winds would die down for a while, he might get one in, but he couldn't plan on it. It was still a long, steep, narrow canyon.

If the winds didn't die down, it wouldn't matter anyway.

It was 4:45 on Friday morning.

*   *   *

BREAKING NEWS FROM CHANNEL 14 NEWS: LOS ALAMOS ON FIRE!

STUDIO: Janet Herrera

"This is Action 14 News, with a Special Morning-Line Report. I'm Janet Herrera, sitting in for Jeremy Edwards.

"The city of Los Alamos is on fire. At 1:30 this morning, Los Alamos was evacuated. All of the work yesterday to build a fire line to contain the fire south of the city literally went up in flames last night as the fire jumped across Los Alamos Canyon and into the city. According to Los Alamos police, the evacuation went very quickly, and the town was declared empty at about three o'clock this morning. Michael Tumbah was there, and we go to him now. Michael?"

REMOTE: Michael Tumbah

"It may be morning where you are, Janet, but there will be no morning here in Los Alamos. We will not see the sun at all today. We are totally engulfed in thick, gray smoke, and I can see ashes and burning embers falling around me, even though I'm miles from where the fire jumped the canyon early this morning. Not many of those embers are landing, though, as you can see by the trees behind me. The winds were just as bewilderingly strong during the night as they have been over the past two days. However, and this is very good news, the winds started dying down about an hour ago. Maybe, just maybe, they'll be able to get the firefighting planes into the air soon.

"Going back to the evacuation, it was at 1:30 this morning that air raid sirens were sounded all over town, along with police and fire sirens, to alert the residents of this community to get out, to leave their belongings behind and get out of town as fast as they could. Here's some film we took very early this morning. You can see bumper to bumper traffic in all lanes as people are leaving behind not only their homes and belongings but, in some cases, their entire lives. The Los Alamos police were..."

STUDIO: Janet Herrera
"Michael. . .Michael?"

REMOTE: Michael Tumbah
"Yes, Janet?"

STUDIO: Janet Herrera
"Michael, let me interrupt you for a moment. We've just made contact with Steve Arquette with the Action 14 News SkyCam helicopter. SkyCam is now airborne for the first time in three days. Steve, can you tell us what you're seeing?"

REMOTE: Steve Arquette [in SkyCam, over Los Alamos]
"Janet, Michael, we've only been in the air for a few minutes. We're relieved that the winds have decreased enough that we were allowed to take off. Only in the last hour have the winds become significantly less than they were yesterday, and that allowed us to receive our clearance to lift off and

move north of the city. We circled the airfield and have now gone up and over the large cloud of smoke and are now coming into the townsite from the west, about where the fire jumped the canyon last night.

"You wouldn't believe what we're seeing here. Let me pull back a bit. . . . It's only been daylight for a few minutes, so the pictures will be pretty dark. The whole city of Los Alamos is absolutely covered in smoke. We launched just minutes ago, just after the sun was coming up. We have to stay far north because of the smoke covering the city and the mountains to the west. . . . I can see some of the streets on the very north edge, I think. We're going to move closer and maybe closer to the mountains, but we have to stay out of the smoke.

"Let's see. . .uh. . .wait, I've got houses. I've got houses. Can you see this, Janet? Let me zoom in here. . .there. Oh, my, there are houses burning . . .three, four. . .are you seeing this? This is the first time that we've been able to. . .there are some more. We'll see if we can hold right here, but we've got houses burning. We're watching whole houses just burning to ashes right before our eyes.

"Janet, Michael, can you tell where these houses are? I'm not sure what street we're looking at, but there's no doubt that houses are being gobbled up by the intense flames and utterly destroyed. Wait. Wait a minute. Hang on for a moment.

"Do you see this? Janet, Michael, I'm not sure what we're looking at. It's a plane, maybe a scout plane, I'm not sure. Did you see the parachute?

Someone, and I have no idea who, but we were just panning north of the city and went up to avoid the smoke clouds, where in the distance—over toward that peak, the peak in the center of your picture—we saw a tiny plane and then something—it looked like something falling from the plane—and then a parachute opened. Right after it opened, it disappeared into the smoke. Michael, has the National Forest Service brought in smokejumpers?"

REMOTE: Michael Tumbah

"Steve, Janet, I was watching the monitor and can't believe what I've just seen. No, as far as I know—though I haven't been in contact with the Command Center in the past thirty minutes—but, no, I've heard of no plans whatsoever to bring in smokejumpers. This isn't their kind of fire. They're used at the beginning of fires, but never, as far as I know, on a fire already this large.

"I'm getting on the phone right now to the Command Center to find out any information, any information whatsoever that they will give us about this event. Now maybe, just maybe, this is part of the rescue effort for the backpacking group that we announced yesterday. That rescue effort has been in the planning stages, and we have not had any update about the rescue status or any other additional information about the fate of those teen-agers who were on a research trip out of the conference center at the Valles Caldera Preserve."

STUDIO: Janet Herrera

"Michael, Steve, please keep us updated on this situation. It seems to be changing by the minute. We're going to switch over now to rerun the Command Center's briefing from midnight last night, when the overall situation was reported. Of course, that was before the fire line was breached and the city of Los Alamos was evacuated."

Jim Daniels' voice boomed across the command center and echoed off the walls.

"FIND OUT WHO THAT JOKER IS, AND GET ME THE PILOT OF THAT PLANE!"

It was 6:11 on Friday morning.

CHAPTER

15

"**D**id you see that?" Mogi yelled into John's ear.

John turned sharply and stopped long enough to see another tree on the ridge burst into flames like a struck match head. His eyes were wide open, full of terror.

"It's like kindling!" Mogi shouted.

John's face was black with soot. Trails of sweat ran down his cheeks, and his eyes were a red-streaked white against his dark face. Mogi could see a reflection of flames in his eyes as he shuddered, turned, and struggled down the trail. The group had stopped only once since they'd started, but the teens could not stand still long enough to catch their breath before they were again rushing ahead.

Having sped up, Mogi stopped to watch the ridge as the others passed by. The trees on the ridge behind them whipped in the wind like dry stalks of grass. Great swirls of ash and smoke boiled into the air around the trunks, and then flames engulfed whole trees in blankets of fire.

"Let's go! Let's go!" Mogi was suddenly shouting as the last of the group passed by. He urged them forward, pointing at Jennifer in the lead and hurrying them to catch up. He hated to yell at them, but he could hardly control his voice. And he was afraid that if he didn't yell, someone would give up, and then he would give up, unable any longer to overcome the despair.

In a few minutes, they spurted up an incline, which sucked the last energy from them but planted them on the top of a ridge. Everyone collapsed onto the trail as Mogi struggled up the last few feet, sucking in as much air as possible over his stifled sobs of exhaustion. Even Jennifer was on her hands and knees, coughing and hacking with her eyes closed.

Catching himself on his way to the ground, Mogi forced himself to stay on his feet. He stood bent over, his sides aching. Just a moment of rest, he thought, just a moment. Maybe two moments.

But no more.

It hurt his throat to yell, but somebody had to do it: "We've got to go! We can't stop now! We've got to get going. Get up and move!"

The yelling had no effect. Eleven ash-covered, dirty, haggard, heaving bodies were collapsed on the trail, watching the flames behind them. It didn't seem fair. All their efforts, all the distance they'd gone.

Mogi finally fell beside his sister, close enough to see the panic in her eyes.

How much farther could it be? They had to be close. They'd hiked up and down at least three inclines, passing above at least two other canyons. They had to be close. He hadn't been able to get his brain relaxed enough to remember the map, but he could recall one portion: He knew the trail split someplace in front of them. One branch went down into the foothills around the city, and the other went on to Guaje Lake.

Jennifer stood and pulled her brother up.

"We've got to go," she said hoarsely.

Mogi stumbled up, yelling at the others.

Where was the split? How far ahead was it? What if he missed it? He didn't want to think about that. He didn't want to think about anything. He just wanted to lie down and quit. It was 6:11 on Friday morning.

Nancy choked back a sob when Muck jumped through the small door of the plane. It was as if that leap snapped the last string of her sanity, the only sure lifeline she had. Now that he was gone, there was nothing more to do. They had broken every rule, every caution against danger, every safeguard created to keep rescue workers safe.

It had taken Nancy and Muck a while to prepare Muck's equipment. He'd laid out the parachutes as carefully and quickly as he could. The chutes were the primary concern—nothing else mattered if they failed. The main one first, and the auxiliary second. He carefully stretched out, smoothed, folded, and then packed each massive fabric into a small, carefully layered package that was cradled into a compact canvas wrap. Muck focused on not allowing even the tiniest mistake, knowing it had been a long time, and that his fingers no longer worked with the confidence of practice.

After the chutes were packed, he checked his clothing: the traditional yellow firefighter shirt with long sleeves, leather-tough pants, and his white boots—the huge, thick-soled, over-the-calf leather boots worn by smokejumpers. Then, just before they took off, he would put on the last layer—the one-piece, pull-on jumpsuit. It was special, made of fire-resistant Nomex and bullet-resistant Kevlar over half-inch, closed-cell foam padding. The Kevlar protected him against punctures by broken branches if he slammed into a tree, or the dangerous spikes sticking out of logs if he had the misfortune of being dragged along the ground.

Into huge pockets around the legs Muck stuffed a hundred-foot letdown rope to lower himself if he was caught in a tree, a set of signal streamers, a large first-aid kit, plastic water bottles, and several emergency fire shelters—large, highly reflective "tents" that could be shaken out by firefighters to crawl inside if they were overtaken by fire.

It was a last measure to stay alive in the middle of a firestorm.

He carried two helmets. One was the size and shape of a motorcycle helmet, with a wire cage over the front. This was his jump helmet. Another, a smaller aluminum helmet like those used in construction, was stuffed into a backpack that was suspended below his waist and strapped between his legs. He'd use that helmet once he was on the ground.

Muck broke a lock off the fuel pump at the airfield while Nancy looked over the plane and ran through her pilot's checklist. After they rolled the plane out of the homemade hangar, Muck ran the fuel line, and Nancy checked the inside. They moved as fast as they could.

The airfield was rough, and strong winds kicked the plane back and forth before it gained enough power to pull into the air. As they turned toward Guaje Lake, Muck made his last preparations, touching every zipper, every pocket, every strap, to make sure all were fastened. With the wind behind them, it wasn't long before they made it to the ridge above the lake.

They could see nothing but smoke. He had hoped for an outside chance to make the lake on the jump; now it would have to be the upper end of the canyon.

He had Nancy circle twice, flying low to see the terrain, though it was mostly hidden by smoke. He threw a couple of streamers to show the air flows. Then it was time to go.

They had removed the passenger door and left it at the airfield. Burdened with a hundred pounds of equipment, barely able to move the big helmet around to see what he was doing, Muck struggled to step through the small opening of the plane.

In all his years of jumping, he had encountered almost every danger possible, and it was a fundamental principal that if smokejumpers do stupid things, they die.

He was now doing stupid things.

Don't jump into smoke, don't jump through a small door, don't jump into hurricane winds, don't jump with an inexperienced pilot, don't jump into the path of the fire.

Gritting his teeth, Muck put his foot in the doorway, grabbed the wing strut of the plane with one hand and the door opening with the other, and flung himself toward the earth.

Dropping like a rock, Muck could make out trees, outcroppings, and bare spots in the forest, but the scene drifted in and out of thick clouds of smoke. His drogue chute was out, dragging behind him and keeping him upright in the air. He had jumped low, to drift as little as possible, so he immediately pulled his release handle, allowing the drogue to pull out his main chute. Unfolding perfectly, the chute was immediately slammed open by the strong winds, sending a jolt through Muck's body.

As he pulled on his directional handles, he found the ride down to be like the Tilt-A-Whirl at a carnival. He did all he could to control his flight, but it was only half enough.

He had wanted to land at the top of Guaje Canyon, right on the bare ridge, but the wind had other ideas, pushing him over the ridge and swirling him into the top of a stand of aspen, dragging him across the top branches like a cheese grater. The limbs thrashed him as he went across. The wind lifted him up out of the trees, back down, and then slammed him into a rock outcropping. He could hear his Kevlar rip as his helmet cracked against the rock.

Muck's eyes strained. He saw stars. He hit his breakaway clips and the chute jerked away from his body. With a last effort as the pain engulfed him, he gave a heave to wedge himself between two rocks. Then he gave up to the pain that swallowed him whole. The lights went out, and he knew nothing more.

It had been a good effort, a brave attempt.

It was 6:13 on Friday morning.

Mogi was surprised that he felt lonely. There were lots of emotions—so much fear that he wanted to cry, an overwhelming desire to lie down and give up, and waves of anger at the others. He wanted to push them out ahead, to make them not follow him. Maybe he felt lonely because he wanted to be alone. He wanted to run and run and run and run and not care about anybody else.

The split in the trail had been obvious; it was well-worn and even had a sign. They darted to the left and found a trail sheltered from the smoke and the wind. Getting their breath back, they settled into a steady pace. The trail, skirting the top of another canyon, was relatively level until it climbed to the next ridge. After half an hour, they struggled up the incline until there was no more up.

Dropping to the ground, wheezing, coughing, furiously wiping their faces clear of soot-filled sweat, they turned to watch the fire behind them as the wind swirled ash and embers around them.

The flames were closer than before.

"It's faster than we are," Henry said with a sad voice, a given-up voice. "It's faster. We can't outrun it." The others heard him and looked across at the flames.

He was right, Mogi thought. That's why it was closer. It was just faster.

"Look! Look!" Henry was suddenly pointing down the east side of the ridge on which they sat.

Fire.

The inferno behind them, the flames that they had been running away from, was only part of the fire. Now that they had turned a corner and gone to another ridge, they could see what had been hidden from them.

A bigger fire was below them, below the steep sides of the mountains and down on the mesas that held the town.

It—it was everywhere. As the teen-agers had raced across the sides of the mountains, the fire had crossed below them, and now smoke was boiling out of the lower end of the canyon in front of them.

But Mogi was sure that the canyon was Guaje Canyon, the canyon that was supposed to be their escape. His stomach churned, and he gagged. Was the fire going to beat them to the lake? Had they run all the way here just to die anyway?

"Where's the lake? I don't see the lake!" John bellowed as he peered over the edge.

Mogi couldn't concentrate. Were they on the wrong ridge? If they had another canyon to cross, they'd never make it.

He needed everything to turn off for a moment, to get quiet, to let him smoothly unfold the map in his mind, find the conference center, trace the route from the parking lot to the trailhead, mark the first ridge with a pen, make a dotted line exactly where they had been, count the ridges, and make positively, absolutely sure where they were in relation to the lake. He needed them to leave him alone so he could be sure.

But they wouldn't quit bothering him. Twenty hands buzzed around him, bodies pushed against him, and everybody was yelling and screaming and crying. Mogi felt the panic rise, and his eyes filled with tears. He couldn't find the ridge. He couldn't find the lake. Everything had become a blur, and now they were all shouting at him.

He shoved his way clear, toppling Charlotte on top of some other guy, and bowling John over into the bushes. He lunged onto the trail, sprinting as fast as he could, stumbling like his legs had come out of their joints, coughing as his face screwed up and he shook all over, trying to scream and cry and yell and breathe all at the same time. He couldn't keep it in anymore.

He was going to burn! They were all going to burn!

The others picked themselves up and raced behind him in full panic. Jennifer, with what little she had left, sprinted after her brother.

The trail moved up the ridge for several feet and then plunged downward. It was downhill but caused no change in the group's motion—everyone kept running as fast as they could. Mogi was still ahead, his long legs flailing as if the devil were chasing him, his hands and arms flopping around his body, his lungs forcing screams from his mouth.

Far beyond any mental control, Mogi leaned his head over too far and lost his footing, his face hitting the hard-packed, rocky dirt. The momentum drove his torso sideways, over the edge of the trail. His legs flew over his body, and he was somersaulting and skidding and falling.

The others slowed in horror as they watched Mogi cartwheel out of control. Slowing up and gingerly half-stepping, half-leaping down the side of the trail, they half-caught themselves and half-caught Mogi until everyone finally slid to a stop. Those far behind slid down to the others and collapsed around them.

No one said anything. Jennifer found her brother and wrapped her arms around him, too exhausted to speak. The others were soon doing the same, their arms linking as if it was one last attempt to stay alive.

Henry raised his head. "Look! Look! Look! The lake!"

There it was, not a hundred feet away. A beautiful blue mountain lake surrounded by tall pine trees, a barren shore of cool mud and reeds, and fringes of marsh grass.

Water. Water. Water.

With whatever energy they had left, overcoming whatever exhaustion they felt, everyone yelled and pushed their way out of the huddle.

Standing, dashing, stumbling, leaping, running—a mess of motion hit the water as if to make a splash that would cover the whole forest.

They had made it!

It was 7:15 on Friday morning, the day without a sunrise.

*   *   *

Jim Daniels listened to the crackling message as it came over the radio.

"Turned back. . .fire on Guaje Ridge. . .canyon run probable. . .turned back. . . ."

He hadn't expected the Blue Team to make it. He knew it was a long shot, and he knew that every man on the team had to agree to quit. That meant the situation was bad, worse than they had expected. They had just not been able to outrun the fire.

If the fire was on Guaje Ridge, then the fire was in Guaje Canyon.

He walked over to the map to study what he had looked at a hundred times. Guaje Canyon—long, steep on both sides, heavily forested, cresting up to almost eleven thousand feet.

A recipe for death.

He went back to his chair, sat down, leaned forward, and buried his head in his hands. He could see it in his mind. It would be what they called a firestorm. The fire starts at the bottom of a narrow canyon. As the fire burns up the canyon, it makes a wind that acts like the bellows of a forge. The fire burns hotter and faster until the burning wood gets hot enough to make the sap act like fuel. The wood doesn't even have time to burn before the sap explodes, making gas. Once there's enough of the gas to ignite, then the gas itself explodes, making an even greater wind that shocks the fire to its hottest, producing even more gasses that blast the trees in front of it. The cycle doesn't end until every last tree is incinerated.

It's like the breath of hell. And those kids would die in it.

Jim raised his head and spoke to the men across the room.

"Call the Yellow Team on the radio, please," he said slowly. "Tell them that the fire is in Guaje Canyon. Tell them to hold below the west ridge of Los Posos Canyon. Do not, I repeat, do not go into Guaje Canyon.

"Rescue is aborted."

He put his head back in his hands.

It was 7:20 on Friday morning.

* * *

BREAKING NEWS FROM ACTION 14 NEWS: LOS ALAMOS ON FIRE!

STUDIO: Jeremy Edwards

"Good morning. I'm Jeremy Edwards, with Action 14 News.

"You are watching live footage from our SkyCam helicopter, high above Los Alamos. An estimated two hundred houses are burning. Dozens of fire departments from all over New Mexico and southern Colorado are on the streets of Los Alamos, battling flames wherever they can. The fire is now in the canyons and mountains north of the town. We continue to hear reports of heroism and bravery from the hundreds of firefighters who have spent the night fighting the fire.

"Let's go to Steve Arquette, reporting to us from SkyCam. Steve?"

REMOTE: Steve Arquette

"Thank you, Jeremy. What we're looking at now is the west side of Urban Street. Fifteen, maybe sixteen homes are nothing but smoldering foundations. We were over Arizona Street a few minutes ago, and the fire has swept through that area like a blowtorch. The flames and smoke kept us from counting the homes on fire in that area. Let me swing the camera. . ."

STUDIO: Jeremy Edwards

"Steve. . .Steve, I need to interrupt you for a moment. We're going to switch over to Michael Tumbah for some breaking news. Michael Tumbah has been on the scene at the incident commander's headquarters in Los Alamos. Michael?"

REMOTE: Michael Tumbah

"Jeremy, Steve, I have just come from a special briefing by the National Forest spokesperson. Before dawn this morning, two special rescue teams of firefighters were sent into the mountains after the group of backpackers, twelve teen-agers who have been trapped in the path of the fire for the last twenty-four hours. Those rescue operations have now been called off. I repeat—the rescue operations have been called off. Those rescue teams going after that group of teen-agers in the high country of the Jemez Mountains just northwest of here have been turned around. The situation was too dangerous for them.

"This could be the biggest tragedy of this fire, Jeremy. We've all been extremely fortunate that, up to this point, there hasn't even been a major injury. But it may now be changing. The teams were not able to get to those teen-agers. There was just too much fire, too much wind, too much rugged forest to get through. We've had no communication with those kids. We don't know where they are or what their condition is, but we have now confirmed that the rescue teams were not able to make it and have been officially turned around. The incident commander, Jim Daniels, did acknowledge that they know the fire reached the teen-agers' last known position and is now beyond it. Everyone is hoping that the group did not stay there but made some effort to escape.

"Jeremy, the special briefing was full of people who were utterly exhausted, and I saw many with tears in their eyes, their hearts absolutely broken over the failure to reach those kids. It was a grim moment. Certainly, our thoughts and prayers are with them."

STUDIO: Jeremy Edwards

"Thank you, Michael. This could be the greatest loss of all. As we have watched these last few days and reported on this extreme disaster, this moment may be the cruelest of all."

It was 7:30 on Friday morning.

CHAPTER 16

Charlotte jumped out of the water as fast as she had jumped in. "It's freezing!"

The others were already soaked, but soon staggered back out and dropped to the ground.

"What do you expect from a high mountain lake fed mostly by snow?" a voice called out from behind them.

The teens turned to find Phil Agnew leaning against a rock. For a moment, no one spoke.

"I thought you went home," John finally said.

"Well, call it a sense of duty, I guess. I decided kids as stupid as you wouldn't be able to find the trail without somebody showing you," Phil sneered.

"No, I think you're just trying to cover up that you're a coward and a bully." The voice came from Jennifer.

Though blackened with soot like the others, Phil's face grew red, and his eyes flashed with anger.

"You're not needed here, Phil," Mogi said with an even voice. "You quit on us, we quit on you. Go your own way. We're making it fine without you."

The effect was dramatic. Phil started shaking, throwing his hands up and stomping back and forth in front of what now seemed a resolute crowd of veterans.

"You. . .you don't know what you're doing. You need me! You need me to get. . .to get out of here. . .I know the trail and you. . .you need me! Get your stuff! Follow me! We have to leave!" His eyes were wild, but the anger and pride had vanished. Mogi looked at his eyes. He's scared, Mogi thought. He's as scared as we are, and he doesn't know what to do.

"You know the fire is in this canyon, don't you, Phil? And you don't know whether to go up the trail or not, do you, Phil? You're as scared as we are, aren't you, Phil?" Mogi didn't sound angry anymore. It was just the truth.

Phil shook his fists at them, continuing to scream, "You need me!" After a few seconds, he stopped and stared at them. Tears made little trails through the dark smudges of his cheeks.

"Go ahead, die," he said. "You're on your own." He turned, stomped back to the rock, threw on his pack, and started up the Guaje Canyon Trail at a full run. He passed the sign marked "Valles Grande." Several others, barely able to get up, made to follow him.

"We need to go, don't we? I mean, I'm not following Phil, but we need to get up the trail, right? We gotta get out of here."

Mogi had focused on getting to the lake and had assumed that they would know what to do once they got there. But from the ridge above, they had seen the fire in the canyon below the lake. He hadn't expected that. He thought they'd be okay if they made it to the lake. He thought there'd be a helicopter or something to meet them. But now there was just the fire below them, and it wasn't going to sit still. It was coming up the canyon because heat rises, and it was going to come faster than they could run.

"I. . .I don't think we can make it," Mogi finally said. "The fire is right down there, coming up this canyon. We saw it from the ridge. Maybe if we were rested like Phil, but I can hardly move. We've run a long way for a long time. It's got to be a long way to get out of this canyon, and it's uphill all the way. It could take us a couple of hours. If we had to stop, we'd be right in the middle of the forest. And we've seen how fast this fire moves."

He swallowed hard. "I just don't think we'd make it."

The questions started with everyone talking at once, their panic returning.

"What do we do?"

"Can we stay underwater until the fire passes?"

"I think we need to go up the trail!"

"How about getting real wet, you know, splashing each other when the fire comes?"

"We can make it up the trail. I'm sure we can! Just give us a few minutes to rest."

"Can we make a raft and get in the middle of the lake?"

Mogi was looking down. What had Muck said about what to do when you don't know what to do? He was trying to remember, trying to cut through all the voices screaming inside his brain.

An explosion echoed up the canyon, a pop like a firecracker. Mogi looked over the lake to the east. The smoke was boiling up, rushing up in big swirls. Like he'd seen on the ridge.

The explosion startled the hikers, bringing a strained silence. It was too close. Everyone understood that the trail was no longer an option.

Listen.

Be aware.

Make do with what you've got.

"Everybody come close," Mogi said as he moved toward the others. "Get close so we can hear each other."

The teens calmly approached and huddled close.

"I don't know what to do," Mogi said. "Maybe we could stay in the water for a while, but not for long because it's too cold, so that's what we'll do only if we can't do anything else. What else can we do? Talk to me. What about a raft?"

"We don't have time to build a raft."

"What about a cave? Can we find someplace to hide?"

"Can we get under rocks? Can we sit on top of rocks?"

"Look over there," John said, pointing at a small meadow of marsh grass next to the lake. "Can we get on top of the marsh grass?"

"That's still in the water. We'd be too cold, but it's better than being under water. We could splash each other, or just submerge if the fire comes."

"What about standing on top of something that's on top of the grass? Could we get some branches and put them on top of the grass?"

"Are there any big rocks surrounded by marsh grass? Could we carry rocks over to the grass? Could we make a stone patio or something?"

There were more explosions, and the air above them was growing thick with darkening swirls of ash and embers. Over the noise of the wind gusts and the explosions, a new, deeper sound was growing. A roar, like a jet engine at take-off.

Make do with what you have.

Mogi closed his eyes and thought about what was around them, what they had inside of them, what they had outside of them. Mogi remembered a show he had seen on TV. Fire shelters. Forest firefighters carry folded shelters with them in case a fire catches them.

The space blankets in their emergency kits!

"OK, listen up," Mogi said as he looked around the circle. "Everybody over to the marsh grass. Get your foil blankets out, the rescue blankets, get them open. Get as close to the water and as far away from any trees as you can. Cover yourself in your blanket.

"Wait, before you do that, dunk yourself in the water. Put on your sweatshirts and jackets. Get everything on yourself that you can, and get it all as wet as you can, and then make a tent around you out of your foil blanket. Tuck the edges around you. Let's go!"

The roar was growing louder. The trees were weaving, shaking, whipping in the force of the wind. The heat had grown, and the explosive popping sounds were closer, much closer.

The teens scrambled around the side of the lake and bounded into the marsh grass. The water was about ankle deep. Eleven foil blankets were soon shaken out.

"Lie together, real tight! Push up next to each other and try to get the blanket edges completely held down!" Mogi shouted as the others splashed themselves. "Fold the ends over to protect your feet and head. Tuck the foil under you—push the edges into the grass if you can!"

They huddled together wrapped in a thin film of silver, hoping and praying in a haze of emotion. Mogi could hear the water from the lake being whipped into the air. His blanket buffeted and moved and was being sucked away from him by the wind, and he wished he had gotten closer to whomever was next to him.

He soon couldn't think about anything but the noise. It was too loud, louder than being next to a jet plane at take-off.

It was hot inside the foil. Mogi reached through the foil slit below him, took handfuls of water from the marsh grass, and threw it against the side of the foil, onto his face, and onto his head. It was so hot! He tried moving his legs to splash the water onto them. He kept on splashing as long as he could.

How many minutes? How long had they crowded together, screaming with their eyes shut tight, holding their breaths as the blankets were whipped back and forth? How long was it that they could hear nothing except the roar?

He didn't know. All he could remember later was that it all suddenly stopped.

The fierce winds, the roar, the shaking—it all stopped.

Slowly raising an edge to look out, Mogi cautiously lifted the blanket as the last of the firestorm swept up the canyon and left the survivors behind. Soon faces peered out, and the shelters were unwrapped and pushed aside, a thick layer of hot ash sliding off around them.

They could only stare, their minds numb.

Everything was black or gray. Another world had taken the place of the one they had seen only minutes before. No color. All the greens and browns and blues were gone. The new world was black and gray and smoke and steam.

It was dark from one side of the lake to the other. All that they had seen before—the heavy forest, the greens and browns and dusty tan of the trail, the thick bushes with the broad oak leaves, the thick pine needles, the blue expanse of the lake—all were gone, leaving nothing but tall, skinny, blackened stumps, a foot-thick layer of ash and coal, and a puddle choked with litter.

The fire had burned everything and then moved on, a dragon ravaging everything it touched. It left only bones—charred, spindly bones that were once trees. Like a thick layer of burnt chocolate icing with black toothpicks stuck in it.

Tree bones. Black tree bones.

The air was hot, but not searing. The survivors knelt in the water-soaked grass that had been their salvation, not noticing that the water that had frozen them only minutes before was now lukewarm. They splashed water all over themselves, some of them kneeling, some wading, all splashing to cool themselves.

They might have been shouting and celebrating for having survived, but they could not. It seemed too sudden, too sad, too high a price to pay. They felt as much sorrow as they felt relief.

The once beautiful lake was dirty, full of ash and coals and burned branches and logs, like something dead, like a campfire soaked with water.

It was hard to breathe, with the ash still whipping into the air, and every breath stank of smoke. A layer of ash was everywhere. Mogi looked around the lake's edge. Big humps in the ash were boulders, he thought, and other humps were probably downed trees or rock outcroppings. He looked at the desolate scene with a stunned understanding of the efficiency of fire.

One of the humps moved.

It moved again, and then shook, the ash falling from it to reveal bright orange. Orange surrounded by a sea of black and gray. The orange hump raised, shook, shook again, and then stood up. A man emerged. A tall, lean man in a yellow shirt.

Muck Jones!

The cries of joy from the hikers were almost as loud as their cries of despair moments before. Everyone was yelling and running and jumping and crying and splashing in the water as they made their way over to the grinning man.

Muck's tears left soot trails on his face as they ganged together, their arms holding each other tight in the midst of jumping and laughing.

"I thought I'd lost you," Muck was saying. "I got here just as the firestorm came over the lake, so I rolled out my shelter and hit the mud on the bank. I saw some silver as I went down. Whose idea was it to use the space blankets?"

Everybody grinned.

"Well," Mogi said, "we all figured it out."

"Good job! We'd better move back to the marsh. The ashes are still hot, and they'll do a job on your feet."

He looked around as they began to walk. "Wait a minute. I only see eleven. There should be twelve. Who's missing?"

Charlotte spoke up. "Phil Agnew ran off and left us. He left us here and went up the trail. Didn't you see him?"

"I had to take a more direct route than the trail," Muck said. "He's a pretty strong kid. If he left here before the fire and ran as fast as he could, he might have made it to the ridge. He shouldn't have left you, though. Why did he leave?"

No one answered.

"Well," Muck said, "we'll get to the details later."

Muck passed around water bottles and candy bars for everyone, though they were pretty melted.

There was no place to sit, so everyone moved back to their places on the grass, using their foil blankets to sit in the shallows of the lake. Being wet was not a problem.

"What do we do now, Muck?" Charlotte asked. Muck had found a boulder in the marsh area, wiped it clean from ash, folded his fire shelter, and sat on it while he cooled his boots in the water. He stared at the sides of the canyon, sometimes looking up the canyon as the smoke continued to boil upward.

"Well," he said, "we'll just make ourselves comfortable and wait for someone to come get us. There's a rescue team just on the other side of that ridge, and I expect they'll be along as soon as the fire burns itself out. They had a couple of tankers flying pretty early this morning, and I believe they covered the ridge like a blanket. I expect that the fire up there is already burning itself out. It was going so fast that it could have actually snuffed itself out.

"After that, they'll send a helicopter to get us, though I doubt it can land down here. That means we'll end up hiking out. I expect, however, that they don't know whether we're dead or alive, so we ought to rig up a signal of some kind."

He seems so calm about this, Mogi thought, as he watched Muck open up his pockets and pull out a rope and three more fire shelters.

"Let's see if we can find a couple of stumps that aren't burning too much, about a hundred feet apart. We'll run a line between them and hang these shelters. A plane should be able to see them from a mile away, so that will let them know we're here."

"Didn't you bring a radio?" John asked.

Muck laughed. "Well, I did indeed bring a radio." He reached into his pack and pulled the radio out, holding it by the antenna: it was only a black lump of metal. "I was a little excited, and I dropped it when I pulled out my shelter," he said with a grin.

Hanging the shelters seemed easy until Mogi grabbed one end of the line, stepped over to a blackened trunk, and sank up to his knees in hot ash. The others laughed as he yelped a string of exclamations and ran back into the water.

After that, it was a contest to see who could come up with the best protection for their feet. One of the girls in Jennifer's team won a clear victory by tearing her foil sheet in half, wrapping them around her feet, and caking the whole thing in mud from the lake. When she emerged from a walk in the hot ash, she was wearing ceramic boots.

Mogi and Jennifer had one end of the line around a tall pine and were trying to tie it as high off the ground as they could without touching the tree, which wasn't so much hot as it had a thin layer of char. Mogi finally put Jennifer on his shoulders and, having accomplished the knot tying, paraded around playing the screaming dragon of Guaje Lake.

Two boys on the other end had attempted at least five knots before they found one that worked.

Muck sat on his rock and laughed at the show.

With the line up, Mogi, John, and Ernie had the job of tying the firefighters' shelters onto the rope in three different places, while Charlotte and Henry held the shelters off the ground. They separated them by about ten feet and opened them to flap in the wind.

Charlotte held a shelter as Mogi attempted to tie it onto the rope. They had picked a place over what he guessed had been a big oak thicket because of several burned branches sticking up from the ash. Not quite reaching the rope and using his foot to clear a place to stand on, his eyes glanced to a strange looking shape that emerged as a layer of ash fell away.

It was round.

Assuming it was a rock, he shoved it with the tip of his mud- and foil-covered boot and pushed more of the ash to one side. It wasn't a rock. He kicked more of the ash to reveal that it was the hub of a wheel. Strips of thick rubber had melted into a ring-shaped blob around the hub, and some kind of pipe was sticking out from the center. What would a wheel be doing all the way out here?

He tried to push it over with his foot, but it was too entangled in what remained of the thicket. Large branches poked through the holes in the hub. In his judgment, it had to be pretty old; the oak thicket had branches a few inches in diameter. The wheel would have needed to be there when the oak was a seedling.

Charlotte held Mogi steady as he stood on the wheel hub and reached the rope. He looped an edge of the shelter over it and used a piece of cord to bind the shelter in place. When he let go, the shelter flapped wildly in the wind.

Bright orange against a canvas of black and gray. He wished he had his phone so he could take a picture.

"Will the fire come back?" John asked as everyone moved back to the marsh grass.

"I don't think so," Muck said quietly. "There's nothing left to burn."

CHAPTER

17

Mogi woke up coughing, leaning over the side of the bed and hacking hard. It took his breath away, and he was afraid he was going to vomit again. They said it would take several days, maybe even weeks, before his lungs would be clear of smoke particles. He lay back, finally caught his breath, and relaxed against the pillow.

Within an hour of the shelters being strung, a spotter plane had circled overhead while Muck gave them a thumbs-up signal. Later, a helicopter came, staying high enough that it didn't blow a storm of ash all over the survivors. It lowered a long line with bags of water and food. The rescue team came down from the ridge several hours after that.

Larger helicopters came next, but they couldn't land anywhere close to the lake, so everyone hiked up to the ridge to where the rescue team had hacked out a landing spot. The medics had brought oxygen bottles with face masks, but it still took a long time to get everyone up the trail. Several hikers struggled and had to be helped by the rescuers.

They flew to Los Alamos Medical Center, where they met an endless parade of doctors, nurses, Forest Service officials, laboratory officials, town officials, the governor, a few senators, newspaper reporters, and TV news people. Everybody in America wanted to know about the "Fire Survivors."

They were a modern miracle.

Mesa Grande was the largest fire in New Mexico' history: More than forty-five thousand acres of forest burned, an estimated 44 million trees reduced to stumps, two hundred homes destroyed, four hundred people homeless, and the streets an ocean of gray-white ash.

Their parents had met Mogi and Jennifer as they came out of the helicopter, and he remembered crying like a baby in his Mom's arms. Like maybe for an hour.

The group stayed in the hospital overnight. Released the next day, Saturday, Nancy and Muck—good ol' Muck—brought the group of twelve teen-agers—Sharon had rejoined them— back to the ranch and moved them into the guest lodge.

The guest lodge, a hotel facility that the ranch owners had built in the '80s, stood about a quarter-mile from the ranch house. It was only one building, but it included a clubhouse-type meeting room with a two-story ceiling, a huge stone fireplace, a big kitchen, and lots of card tables and leather-covered sofas. It had two wings with sixteen bedrooms, each with a bathroom. Built as a rental facility for visiting groups, mainly corporate management meetings and retreats, the business had thrived until the economy tanked in the late '90s.

For the teen-agers, it felt like a high-dollar resort.

As a last ceremony, the rest of the camp had a big lunchtime celebration for the Fire Survivors, and there were more TV cameras and helicopters than the day before. The teens were exhausted, though, and Nancy finally chased them into the lodge and forbade them to leave. Sleep as much as you can, drink lots of fluids, yada, yada, yada.

The rest of the camp attendees packed up and were gone by the end of the day on Saturday. It was nice to finally be left alone. Mogi grew tired of watching himself and the others on TV, saying the same things over and over again, but he felt his heart jump into his throat whenever he saw a photo or watched a video of the fire.

In between naps, he and Jennifer relaxed in the comfy chairs of the big room.

"You did good," she said. "We all did good."

"Yes, we did, and we were lucky," Mogi replied as his body shuddered. Muck said that body shakes were not unusual. The shuddering would stop as they rebalanced their bodies with food and sleep. And time.

Mogi needed time for his body and his mind to put away the terror he had experienced.

"Did your dreams come back last night?" he asked his sister.

"Not as bad as the night before. I'm learning to quiet myself down and go back to sleep," Jennifer replied. "I still see faces, though. Eyes big with fear, faces shaking with terror, faces with tears making streaks down the cheeks. And I see you doing screaming cartwheels down the side of the mountain."

The rescue team had seen another teen-ager at the top of Los Posos Canyon moments before the firestorm choked off the top of Guaje Ridge. He was covered in a fine layer of the red, sludgy fire retardant dropped by the fire bombers. They tried to stop him, but he was running so fast that he made it through them before they realized it.

No one had seen or heard from Phil after that, but his belongings that were stored at the ranch disappeared sometime on Friday. Muck figured he got his stuff, made it to the highway, and hitchhiked back home. The conference center was trying to track him down, but had had no success.

The forest fire was still burning and was expected to burn for a long time, but it had descended out of the high country into flatter lands that had thinner forests and smaller trees. It was now far to the north of the city and would eventually burn itself out.

The dragon had been tamed and would be back asleep in a few weeks.

The survivors were asked to stay on a few days. An investigative team was coming from U.S. Forest Service headquarters in Washington, D.C., and wanted to interview them. Only a handful of people had ever lived through an actual firestorm. To accommodate the schedule, the survivors' parents were treated to free housing and food, compliments of the conference center and the lab. The parents got the dorm and the cafeteria while their children got the guest lodge.

It was past noon on Sunday when Mogi had awakened with his hacking cough. He pulled the sheet back—a clean, pure white, cotton sheet—marveling at how nice it felt. In spite of taking two showers on Friday and three on Saturday to get the soot and grime out of his pores and his hair, he still smelled like an old barbeque grill.

Broad rays of sunshine came through the large window in his room, beyond which lay the pastures. It was almost one o'clock.

Wow. He was *still* sleeping a lot.

He dressed and wandered downstairs. Charlotte was in the big room, sprawled out on the sofa, asleep, but woke as he came down.

"Hey," she smiled.

"Hey. Where is everybody?"

She sat up. "Well, the staff and our parents are getting a special tour of the burned areas in town. I think your mom and dad went with them. Everybody's gone but us 'survivors'. We're still confined to the ranch, which is fine with me." She lay back down and stretched.

"I guess Ernie and Henry are still upstairs—I haven't seen them. John was down for breakfast, but then he went somewhere. They let Sharon go into town. I'm not sure what the other team is doing. What are you going to do?"

"Oh, I'll just wander. Did you say breakfast? Where do I find some food in this place?"

She laughed. "You're on your own, but the refrigerator looks pretty full."

Mogi found the makings for a couple of sandwiches, wolfed them down, and was working on his second Dr. Pepper when he went outside. It was a beautiful day, completely clear except for a gathering of dark clouds above the peaks of the mountain range to the east.

Mogi's heart began to pound. He looked at the clouds for a long time, trying to remember how regular clouds looked compared to columns of smoke. Finally, he was sure they were clouds and not smoke. He took a deep breath. He'd had enough smoke for a lifetime.

He wandered around the lodge, down to the corrals to watch the horses for a few minutes, and then over to the conference center. There were several cars in the parking lot, but no sounds of people. He passed by and went around the corner.

The big door to the equipment room was down, but unlocked. He raised the door. Finding Muck's office open, he went in and sat down.

He didn't have his conference notebook, but there was a pad of paper in the desk drawer and a pen. Writing deliberately, but as fast as he could to keep up with his mind, Mogi emptied his memory onto the pages. He needed to sort it all out.

He wrote everything about the program—the hikes, the fossils, Fenton Lake, wading in the creek after fish, the horseback ride. He wrote what he remembered, in sequence, filling five pages.

He wrote everything about the mystery—the visit to the museum, Nancy's outrage, the story of the plutonium theft, the box of Nancy's stuff, the Russian professor. Of course, the story's ending had been cut short. He knew about the plane, so clues didn't matter any more. End of the road.

There was still the Morse code message, though, but it must have just been an accident, or the power lines, like they said. The radio would never have been able to broadcast from inside a truck in the canyons north of the mountain range. End of the road.

He wrote everything about the fire.

He felt his eyes tear up and his throat thicken, and he shuddered again. He couldn't help it. He tried to list out the happenings as he remembered them, but he had to stop to wipe the sweat from his forehead. He would start a new sentence, and his hand would start to shake while his body shuddered. He stopped, sat back, and took a deep breath, still shaking enough to make the chair squeak.

He forced himself to write.

The ride to town with Nancy, how small the first cloud of smoke looked. The equipment room and Muck's office. Getting his backpacking equipment. The trailer, and starting up the trailhead. There was the hike over the first ridge with Hank, when Sharon was sick but didn't say anything. Hank and Sharon going back. Waiting, waiting, waiting, and then back to the ridge. Jennifer grabbing the snacks. Pain-in-the-rear Phil, and then more waiting, and finally his and Jennifer's hike back to the ridge.

The flames leaping from the top of the ridge, the feeling of absolute terror, the desperation to escape.

The pen fell out of his hand. He couldn't hold it.

Taking deep breaths, closing his eyes, remembering slowly so it wouldn't scare him, he backed his mind up and began again. Each scene returned, and his memory filled in the blanks. But he could not write it down.

Phil, the plane.

They took the plane apart and put it in a truck and drove the truck away. End of the road. End of the story. End of the mystery.

Except. . .

Mogi remembered the picture of the makeshift airfield. There were tracks, but nothing special about the tracks. If there had been a big truck with no plane and then a big truck with a plane inside, the tracks would have been deeper, much deeper. Somebody would have noticed.

How many minutes to take the wings off an airplane?

Why worry about taking the plane at all?

Mogi relaxed and his hand stopped shaking.

Focus.

Whoever it was, they'd know that whatever they did would be discovered by daylight. Why not just leave the plane? Or fly it away, far away from the cars so that the search would be divided?

In fact, a big truck would have been slower than flying the plane. So why take the plane?

Wait a minute. They didn't even take the lanterns! They were not worried about being discovered. The plane would have been obvious from the beginning, so who would care if they left it or took it?

Phil was wrong.

The government's position was that there were no good guys. Everyone, the pilots included, were all bad guys stealing plutonium. But if they were all bad guys, why land the plane at all? Why not just fly the plane farther away? The field was created for the plane to land, so they obviously meant to put the plutonium in the cars and make a run for it. It would be easy to switch to different cars later. Given that, the plane becomes meaningless to them and maybe even a burden. They'd leave it at the field.

But the plane wasn't left at the field. Someone must have flown it away from the field, which means there was at least one good guy. And if a good guy had flown the plane away, he'd want to get the plane back to the airport, and he'd try to contact the airport as he was doing it.

Mogi pulled the copy of the logbook message from his wallet, along with the listing of Morse code he had written down.

There are too many dots and dashes in the logbook's sequence, so it's Morse code gibberish. But suppose that instead of looking for all the words, you looked for only one word.

Like "HELP."

He picked up the pen and wrote.

H is four dots; E is one dot; L is a dot, a dash, and two dots; and P is a dot, two dashes, and a dot.

The first thing he needed was six dots in a row.

He found them. In fact, there were seven. He grouped the first four together, and then looked for a dot, a dash, and two dots. Ignore anything in between. He found them, following the next two dots. One dot must be extra, Mogi thought.

A dot, two dashes, and a dot. They were next, but there was an extra dot between them and the previous letter.

There's an extra dot between each word, Mogi realized. It may have been static, but if you took each of them out, it spelled H E L P.

Mogi looked at the dots following the letters he had found. Suppose the radio was broken or something and was inserting dots or dashes or blanks on its own. Like maybe every time the sender paused, the radio set burped or something.

Mogi looked for another word.

What else would have been in the message? What else would a pilot in trouble spell out if he couldn't talk on the radio? Think!

His location.

But I don't know the location! I don't even have a guess. But, maybe. . .

His name.

Mogi wrote down the two names—SAMPLES and JOHNSON—and wrote them in Morse code:

. . . . - - - . . - - . . . - . . . . - - - -
- - . . . . - . . . . - - - - .

He inserted dots between each of the letters:

. . . . . - . - - . . . - - . . . - . . . . - - -
. - - - . . . . - . . . . . - - - . - .

He looked over the message. He didn't find a string of eight dots, but he did find seven. And there was a series of . . .

He started decoding from the dots backward, and then forward. **H. . .O. . .J. . .N. . .S. . .O. . .N. . .**

JOHNSON

Wow!

He focused on the other dots and dashes, carefully marking off what would have been letters and what would have been extra dots.

He finished and sat back in the chair, stunned at what had emerged.

The message repeated itself. Over and over, someone desperately trying to communicate.

The pilot was telling where he was taking the plane.

CHAPTER

Above the mountains of Northern New Mexico
August 24, 1963

I t was the deep black of a night with no moon; dawn was a half-hour away. In the glow of the tiny dials and lights of the dashboard, Major Henry Samples looked calm, but Chris Johnson knew that Henry's heart was beating into his throat just like his own. After the horror of the other plane's crashing into the ground below, they had dropped in altitude and turned to the west as they were told.

The cold steel barrel against his neck kept Chris silent.

"Over the north end of Abiquiu Lake, south to 34, and then follow it. Stay about two hundred feet above the road." The third man's voice was even and professional.

The guy was crazy. Two hundred feet above the ground wasn't much in this mountain country. Add in variations in the terrain like hills, arroyos, canyons, and hundred-foot trees, and it was like flying across the top of a jiggling black soup.

The small plane slipped into the electronic shadow of the mountains where no radar could penetrate and flew over a scattering of houses. Only a few hundred people lived within a fifty-mile radius, a perfect country for disappearing.

It was ten minutes more before "Bill" pointed them toward a dark pasture ahead. A row of dim lanterns lay out a landing strip.

Continuing to hold his gun in the direction of the pilots, the third man removed his seat belt and used his left hand to unbuckle the straps securing the yellow cases. With the straps undone on the first one, he cautiously stood, hunched over in the small cabin, and moved to the cabin door. He jerked the handle and opened it as the plane cut back its engines for the landing. Below, five or six vehicles parked along the makeshift runway turned on their headlights, spreading a surprising amount of light across the darkness.

Henry Samples touched the plane down with shakes and jolts as it hit the bumps of the uneven dirt surface. Leaning loosely against the sides of the plane for the landing, the man in the back of the plane turned to look at the cars at the side of the airstrip.

As if waiting for that moment, Henry threw the throttles fully forward and jerked the wheel back. The man went sprawling.

"Get this plane out of here!" Henry yelled at Chris as he threw off his seatbelt and lunged over his seat onto the man who was now flailing on the cabin floor. As Henry wrestled the man, Chris put his strength into controlling the bouncing plane and hoped there was enough pasture left to get the plane into the air.

There wasn't.

Its engines roaring, the plane had bucked off the last high spot when it caught the barbed wire of a fence. Chris heard the rasp of the wire as he angled upward, a sharp ratcheting sound like a buzz saw, and felt the jerk as the wire pulled at the plane.

Acting like the sharp teeth of a chainsaw, the wire shredded the wheel struts and left one wheel clinging by only a thin piece of aluminum. In the glow of the headlights below, Chris watched the loose wheel disappear toward the ground. A red landing gear light flashed on, and Chris knew that the plane could not land again.

With a last savage gesture at losing the battle, the wire whipped upward and ripped a foot-long cut into the left wing. A severed fuel line shot a spray of gas over the front window.

A shot rang out, and then another, and another.

Henry Samples slumped behind the seats, a hoarse, spitting groan passing his lips. Wrestling the gun away, Henry had taken a bullet to the chest before he had turned the pistol and got off two rounds into the body of the man.

Chris struggled against the controls. The barbed wire shredding the wing was bad enough, but now the cabin door was open, making it much more difficult to keep the plane from swerving all over the place.

As Henry groaned, the man struggled to reach the back door, dragging the yellow case. He clutched it as he fell out the door.

The plane was a hundred feet above the ground when a scream cut through the darkness.

Chris felt two sharp pains in his leg and realized that the people on the ground were shooting at him. He screamed as much as he could without losing his presence of mind, but it gave only temporary relief. In a few seconds, he felt the warmth of the blood against his trousers.

He focused on the controls, gaining altitude and making a sweeping left turn.

Over the mountains, he thought. Back home, I've got to make it back home!

He moved one hand down and tried to find a pressure point on his leg, but he didn't have the strength to stem the flow.

The smell of blood mixed with the smell of gunpowder and airplane fuel. Gasping in the foul air, reeling from the pain, he vomited.

Spitting, gagging, panting as the waves of pain increased in his body, Chris heard a tiny voice. In all of the panic, bullets, and blood, his headphones had remained on and he was hearing the faint voice of the Los Alamos airport dispatcher.

He yanked the handset from the console and yelled into it. But his thumb touched only jagged metal and wiring instead of the button, and what remained of the microphone hung in his hand. Half of the handset had been blown away by a bullet from below, maybe even the bullet that had passed through his leg.

The gas is leaking. I'm dying. The enemy is watching. My radio is dead.

A shudder of despair went through him, but years of experience forced him to discipline his thoughts.

The radio wasn't dead, but his handset was.

The radio dial on the console glowered back at him, and the tiny, urgent voice kept calling.

A wave of weakness swept over him as he tried to piece together the sounds. The voice was urgent, but he couldn't make out the words.

Chris pressed his thumb against the jagged metal and heard a crackling in his earphones. He pressed it several times and heard the static each time. For every press of his thumb, there was a corresponding hesitation in the voice on the other end. Maybe the guy was hearing something.

Chris pressed the button up and down, working hard to remember his Morse code.

The airplane bucked, jerking him in his seat, and he reeled through another wave of nausea.

He was losing altitude. He dropped the handset and pulled back on the controls, felt the plane shudder as it began to climb, and then looked at the stars.

Where am I?

Everything below was pitch black, but he could see the difference between the grassy pastures and the dark of the forest. He was in the mountains for sure, but where? No matter how far, he needed to go east. The town was east, but so were the mountain peaks.

One of the last glowing lights on the instrument panel blinked a bright yellow: Low fuel.

Oh, great.

He turned the volume up on the microphone to hear the crackle more clearly, and again picked up the handset. Listen to me, he thought, listen to me! He continued to key in his message.

The yellow, blinking low fuel light turned a solid red.

He was done for. He was going down just as soon as he ran out of the cupfuls of fuel hidden by the gauge.

Where to go, he kept asking himself. Where? If I hit the ground, the plutonium goes all over creation, and the land will be poisoned for years. I need to put it down in one piece. But I have no wheels.

Mary's going to be angry over this. We never talked about her becoming a widow.

He stared desperately out the window. Where was he? The glow of the barest beginnings of sunrise came from the east, and against it he could see the peaks. He had flown over the Jemez Mountains dozens of times, and he knew the peaks by heart. If only he could get a good look.

Afraid of losing any more altitude than needed, he turned the plane enough to see the outlines of the peaks. One, two, three.

OK. He knew where he was, and he remembered how often he deliberately flew over the beautiful mountain lake on the other side of the ridge.

The lake.

That would be good enough. It had to be good enough. If he could make the lake, he'd come across the water long ways, drag the tail, kill the engines, and slide in on his belly. The plane would stay together, and the water would keep any fire from melting the cases. He might even be able to run it up on the shore.

He started his finger on the handset button again, this time slower, struggling to remember how to spell the words.

I've got to let them know.

He franticly pressed the words into the handset. Over and over.

Seeing the mountains coming closer, he pulled back on the controls, carefully balancing going up with going forward to keep from stalling the plane. There was a dip between the peaks, a ridge along the tops of the canyons of the eastern slope. Over that ridge, and he'd be on a down run to the lake.

His lower leg had gone numb, but the ache in his thigh changed to stabbing pain as he shifted his weight to steady himself against the vibrations of the wounded plane. His right foot slopped in a shoe filled with blood.

With his head against the side window, he strained to follow the dim outline of the mountains against the far sky and, when he saw the dip, threw the plane into a sharp right turn. The plane struggled, then floated as it lifted over the exposed rock of the ridge. The engine coughed, chugged, and then coughed again.

Chris's eyes closed for a brief moment. Mary, sweet Mary. Maybe he'd take her dancing tonight, and to a nice restaurant. She'd like that.

What shall we name the baby?

Christopher Johnson passed out and slumped in the seat.

The plane pitched downward and slid across the treetops, first bending the branches and then shearing them off like a scythe, but the layers of branches in the thick forest kept the plane upright. What was left of the landing gear plowed through the crowns of the trees, caught, and then ripped free from the plane, yanking away what the barbed wire fence had pulled loose. Catching the thick trunk of a tall pine tree, the plane flipped, its tail catching the edge of the water and catapulting the plane onto its belly.

With a wallop, the plane slid over the surface of the water until it was grabbed by the wave of water shooting up in front of it. With one wing tipping into the lake's surface, the plane spun violently sideways and shuddered to a rocking stop.

Rushing, slapping, sucking, the water swallowed the intruder. The weight of the engine pulled the front of the plane downward and kept it in a slow sinking motion as the air whooshed out the broken windows and up through the cargo door.

The tail stood alone with a final bob, then slipped beneath the surface. The black mud and silt, swirling up from the bottom in protest, wrapped the plane in the darkness of the churning water. In less than two minutes, the remaining air escaped its prison, and the gurgling died away.

Within moments, the high mountain lake returned to the quiet serenity of the early dawn.

CHAPTER

19

Present Day

HELP
JOHNSON
MARSHALL LAKE

Mogi leaned back in his chair, astonished at the message. He slowly gathered up his papers, tapped them into a neat pile, and stood up. He closed Muck's cage, pulled down the equipment room door, and went back to the ranch house.

Charlotte was asleep on the sofa. He quietly made his way up the stairs and into his room. He didn't want to see anybody.

He sat on the edge of the bed.

He was remembering Nancy's look when he'd asked about the third person. She wanted him to quit because he had become too involved—he was getting carried away with it—and probably because she knew he was going to end up making a fool of himself.

Now he seemed to have decoded a message that the smartest people in the world had looked at for a bunch of years and never figured out. Out of the blue, in less than a week, he comes along and thinks he knows what it says. While he was at it, he should have come up with a cure for cancer.

Mogi sat quietly for a while longer, numb, thinking nothing. He felt tired, so tired. It was time to go home.

His eyes wandered around the room. It was a nice room, big and comfortable. There were several pieces of Southwest art: a picture of cowboys on the wall, an Indian blanket over each of the nightstands, a carved headboard with a Zia symbol in it.

On the floor next to the nightstand was Nancy's box. Someone must have brought it from his dorm closet with his clothes. He needed to return it to Nancy.

Should he tell her about the Morse code message? Probably not. Let it go—that's what she had said. It's been fifty years. Let it go. Hasn't the fire been enough excitement for the week? Forget about the message. It doesn't matter. Let it go.

It felt, again, like he was in a rush to be a fool.

Mogi leaned back onto the mattress, stretching his back, taking a deep breath. It felt so good.

What kind of guy was Chris Johnson? Mogi thought. I bet he would have been a good dad to Nancy. And Nancy would have been a good daughter to him.

What did Phil do with the photograph he had taken? Mogi couldn't imagine his being interested in it. He probably threw it away.

How deep would a lake have to be to hide a plane? He remembered that the lake water wasn't clear like in the beer commercials. It was murky, fed with the stain of the decomposing leaves and needles of the forest. You could look at it all day and not see anything.

Mogi coughed hard, turning sideways and hacking, still tasting ash and smoke.

Regaining control, taking a breath, he laid against the cover and sheet, stretching his arms to the side. It felt good to lay back, to feel the softness, to feel the clean, to touch the fluff of the cover.

The photo that Phil took. Mogi closed his eyes to see it with his mind.

One plane was close, while the second plane was in the background. People were working. One, two, three people in addition to Henry Samples and Chris Johnson. Henry was looking at the tail. Chris stood next to the open door, looking inside. The other people were bringing things in or maybe taking things out—jacks, lifts, dollies, some ropes and straps. Big barrels stood in one corner, a few ladders next to them, some toolboxes along the back wall. Most hangars look like this, he thought, with lots of planes being wheeled in and out.

Wheels.

Mogi remembered the two landing wheels on the bottom of the plane. Several inches of rubber around a big, shiny metal hub.

His eyes flashed open.

A shiver started in Mogi's toes, moved up his legs, up his backbone, and shook his whole body. It shook his body so hard that he started hacking and coughing again and had to stand up and bend over to get it all out before he could take a deep breath.

He grabbed Nancy's box and quickly sorted through the folders, finding another photograph that showed the planes. He looked at the wheels—several inches of rubber around a big, shiny metal hub.

A hub just like the one in the ashes at Guaje Lake. He had stood on it.

Mogi felt beads of sweat form on his forehead.

What a time to not have his phone! He didn't have a picture, so he closed his eyes again and remembered.

He had first noticed something round and then tried to kick the ash off of it. It didn't do much good because the ash was so deep. But he could still see it. Maybe he had a seen a tread? The rubber had melted, so it was no longer perfectly round, but the shape of the wheel, the size, the metal hub. . .

Maybe you can look at a series of dots and dashes and make guesses and put them into some sort of order and interpret something out of nothing, and you could be entirely wrong because you were wanting it to say something so bad that you made it come out that way, but there was no way—no way!— that you can make a wheel appear out of nowhere.

The pilot had made it to the lake and probably crashed into the trees. A wheel ripped off and the rest of the plane slid into the lake. That's why they never found any wreckage.

He recalled the Morse code message. Whoever was piloting the plane must have known he was going to crash and had flown the plane right into the lake. That's where the plane is. For more than fifty years, it's been right under everyone's noses.

The door of the room slammed back against the wall as Mogi hit the hallway and headed for the stairs.

"I know where the plane is!" he yelled as he rushed into the living room.

Charlotte's eyes were dazed as she jerked up from a deep sleep. "The airport?"

"No, no, no! The plane that Nancy's father was in, the plane with the plutonium, the plane. . ."

Charlotte's eyes were glazed over.

"Remember the wheel in the ashes? The wheel we found when I was tying on the shelter?"

Charlotte's head formed something like a nod.

"It was from a plane. A plane that's been missing for fifty years!" Mogi was dancing and jumping around as Charlotte tried to understand his raving.

"What in the world are you yelling for?" Jennifer asked as she walked into the room. "I heard you all the way down the hall."

"I found the plane, I found the plane, I found the plane!" Mogi chanted.

"What plane?"

Mogi sat down and explained how he'd solved the Morse code problem and now realized the meaning of the wheel hub in the forest. He even ran back to his room to get the notes he had made in Muck's office.

"You need to tell the Russian professor," Charlotte said in a weary voice. "He was here this morning, before lunch. He wanted to know more about the wheel."

Mogi suddenly had a coughing fit and took a moment to catch his breath. "How did he know about the wheel?" he finally asked.

"Oh, in some interview yesterday or the day before, you know, when everybody was asking questions, and we were telling about what happened."

There had been a lot of interviews. Mogi could hardly remember anything that was said since there were so many people and so many questions.

"I said that we had found this wheel and had stood on it to string up the flags so everybody knew we were alive and everything. The professor remembered and came here to ask more about it. I told him what it looked like after we knocked the ashes off of it. I said he should probably stay and wait for you, but he got this look in his eye and said that he didn't need to see you anymore. He left and that's the last I've seen of him."

Charlotte's words hit Mogi like a slap in the face.

Pistol's words pounded in his brain—nothing is a coincidence. The Russian shows up again, now a third time, out of the blue, asking about a wheel, and. . .

The professor knew. He had figured it out.

No, that's not right. Pistol's an idiot. They don't do things like that anymore.

Oh, yeah? He could hear Pistol's voice. Oh, yeah? They did it then and they do it now, and don't be surprised if they're doing it to you, too.

Mogi couldn't stop the feeling of fear growing inside him. He paced up and down the living room muttering as Charlotte yawned.

Jennifer sat in a nearby chair watching her brother argue with himself. It was something she'd seen before, but now he was acting really mental. They had just barely survived a forest fire, which had to be the most stressful thing they'd ever experienced. Maybe her brother was having flashbacks that he couldn't handle.

If he starts drooling, she thought, I'm calling for help.

When somebody is lying, everybody is lying, Mogi was thinking. The Soviets didn't get the plutonium because something went wrong with the hijacking. They never had the plutonium because the pilots had escaped with the plane. The suitcases in the warehouse picture *were* fake, and they didn't have any more of an idea than we did what happened to the plutonium. So they've been waiting. All these years, they've been waiting.

And I come along and tell them where it is.

I've got to stop it, one way or other, Mogi said to himself as he flew out the front door.

Jennifer ran after him.

Charlotte yawned again, slumped over on the sofa, and went back to sleep.

CHAPTER

20

Mogi leaned over the saddle, urging the horse forward. Muck was going to explode all over him, and it was doubtful that Nancy would ever speak to him again. He had stolen a horse. And a saddle, a saddle blanket, a halter—all that stuff. And he was currently racing like crazy across the main pasture, which meant that he had disobeyed his confinement to the lodge.

"Are you nuts?" Jennifer had said. "The professor is not a spy! Where did you ever get that idea?"

The argument happened as he was saddling the horse in the barn.

He knew she wouldn't understand. She hadn't been thinking about it all week. She hadn't noticed the sudden visits by the professor. She hadn't worked through what a couple of hundred pounds of plutonium could do.

"I've got to go," he told her. "I've got to see what's happening."

"You really believe what you've told me? You think you're going to find helicopters?"

He hesitated. "I don't know what I'll find, but the plane is there, and Nancy's dad's body is there, and I've got to expose any attempt at taking it all away."

He had thrown himself into the saddle and raced toward the trailhead that would take him back to Guaje Lake, leaving Jennifer helplessly behind.

The smell in the wind coming across the meadow was rich with water. Even when the rest of the landscape was starved for water, the conference meadows, fed by springs and streams, grew a lush, deep green grass. The clouds above the peaks, small when Mogi had looked a couple of hours ago, had joined together and now stretched the length of the mountain range. The tops of the clouds were billowing up, and the bottoms were dark.

What a funny twist. An absolutely bone-dry, drought-cursed forest that had burned like crumpled paper was going to make it rain.

The weather forecaster on one of the TV stations had made a big deal about it over the past two days. It had to do with the tremendous heat still coming from the burned surfaces. With the resulting currents of air rising straight up into the atmosphere and meeting the moisture in the upper air, it was likely to rain directly above the burned areas.

The problem with it raining over a burned area is that ash doesn't absorb water; it sheds water. When rain falls on a sloping forest floor covered in ash, raindrops will hit, slide off, join other drops, and the water will keep sliding off, down the slopes, down the ravines, down the canyons and, by the time it gets to the bottom, it's a tidal wave of black water full of ash, cinders, and dirt. Whole trees could be uprooted as the water sweeps through.

A few days ago, everyone was worried about fire; now everyone was worried about floods.

The sounds of the hooves were muffled in the grass. He was remembering Wednesday when he couldn't get the trail horse to do anything. He must have stolen a better horse—this one was flying!

He had looked at the map hanging in the barn. He was headed for Los Posos Canyon, the back way into Guaje Lake. He knew that there had been no fire on that side of the ridge, so the trail should be open. He'd ride the horse as far as he could, hike up to the top of Guaje Canyon, and down the canyon to the lake.

Then what?

He wasn't sure. The cloud cover was perfect camouflage for the Russians to get to the lake, find the plutonium, and get out before anyone knew what was happening. They'd probably use a really fast attack helicopter, with those combat guys that slide down the ropes. In and out before anybody knew.

The important thing is that he had his phone back. He could hide in the trees and take all the pictures he wanted. It wasn't like he was going to try to wrestle the cases out of their hands or anything. All he needed was pictures. Then he could show Nancy and the other people at the lab about what was happening. The Air Force would send fighters, and they'd take those helicopters out in no time—force them to the ground before they got out of U.S. airspace and get the plutonium back. They'd probably be headed to Mexico, since that was the closest border.

Mogi was feeling good. Really good. He had wanted to quit when he discovered the Morse code message. It seemed impossible, so he had to be wrong. But the wheel—the wheel cinched it. Now he knew the solution to the mystery for sure. He was feeling really, really good.

He hadn't meant to run off on Jennifer like that, to leave an argument without listening to her, but she didn't understand. This was something he had to do, and nobody else could do it.

He looked back to see how far he'd come.

In the distance was another rider. It wouldn't be surprising since the ranch hands had to be working today, but there was no question that this rider was following him.

Mogi slowed the horse to a trot and stopped, reining the horse around to face the rider that was charging toward him.

It was still a good distance. He strained to make out the shape. It was a skilled rider on a fast horse, he thought, though he doesn't look like anybody I know. He doesn't have a cowboy hat, only a ball cap, and it's on backwards, and it's. . .

Mogi's heart froze, and he started coughing again.

It was Phil Agnew.

Mogi turned his horse and kicked him into a gallop. No matter what Phil wanted, it wasn't going to be good. He must have been hiding out on the ranch, waiting and watching. Maybe he was psychotic or something.

He led the horse out of the vast pasture, through a scattering of trees, and then into another meadow. Ten minutes more and Mogi saw the sign for the Los Posos Canyon trailhead. He came into a small dirt parking lot and then turned the horse up the trail. Looking back across the meadow, he could see Phil bending low, riding fast.

Mogi hoped the trail in front of him would be like the Guaje Lake trail they had taken on Thursday. If it was, he should be able to ride to the top.

Not more than a mile later, the trail crossed a series of rock outcroppings, and the horse refused to go on. Mogi jumped off the horse, slapped him on the rump, and the horse took off back down the trail.

It was a footrace now.

Raindrops hit the trail in front of him, reminding him again of his lack of preparation. He had brought no rain gear, no jacket, and no water. Since he had to stop periodically to hack and cough, he could really use that water.

But he could see the top of the ridge, so it couldn't be that far. Crossing over to the trail that the group had hiked on to get to the helicopter, he knew it was all downhill, which should allow him to run as fast as he wanted to.

"Hey, dweeb!" a voice shouted from behind him.

Mogi had run as fast as he could, uphill, and was now leaning over, heaving deeply, coughing and hacking like crazy, trying to get a breath. Phil was about three hundred yards behind him, but he was struggling to keep going, too. Mogi could hear him coughing.

Phil couldn't have learned any of the revelations of the afternoon, so he wasn't thinking plutonium or Russians or airplane in the lake. He must only be thinking about Mogi and his insulting sister, and his embarrassment at the lake, and a list of other disappointments in his life, all of which he was going to take out on Mogi when he caught him.

Finally getting a deep breath, Mogi pretty much ran the rest of the trail. Once he got to the ridge and started into the canyon, it was harder to find the trail than he'd expected; the wind must have filled in the footprints the hikers had made. The whole area looked like the aftermath of a war, like the scene he first saw as he peeked out from beneath his foil blanket. Black and gray. The color of death.

It began to sprinkle. The ash was still hot—very hot. When hit by raindrops, it burst into steam, making a ghostly mist that blended with the smoke that was still rising from the burnt layers of bark on the trees. Looking down from the ridge, it appeared as if a fog were coming in from the ocean.

As Mogi plowed his way through the ash, hoping he was on the trail, the rain began for real. Small drops, big drops, a million drops. Little rivers of water were forming everywhere. When a little river broke through the ash surface, puffs of smoky mist hissed into the air.

"I've been waiting for you, dweeb!" the voice behind him called. "I've been waiting so you and I can have a talk."

Mogi plunged ahead into the foot-thick layer of ash, high-stepping his feet as fast as he could. Sloshing his way forward, his feet burned like they had two days before. He was lucky the rain was coming harder, turning the ash into a slime that was at least cooler.

But the rain also made it slippery. Every few steps, he slid down into the mire.

Phil wasn't doing any better, cursing and yelling a blue streak behind.

Mogi struggled to find the energy and the air to keep going. If it hadn't been for Phil constantly yelling his taunts, Mogi would have slowed and taken more time. As it was, he was pushing himself, torturing himself to get down.

It took longer than he expected, but the lake finally appeared out of the mist, a faint opening in the gray and white, maybe a hundred yards away. Now he had to worry about the Russians. He did not want to slide right into the middle of their operation.

Mogi went sideways from the trail, staying low, hoping the rainfall would hide him, that it would cover his tracks. He hoped the haze and smoke would keep Phil from seeing him.

Mogi slid into the slime behind a tree stump and stopped all motion.

Phil appeared out of the fog, looking confused, trying to figure out where his target had gone. Cursing, flailing around in a fruitless search for his prey, yelling at the rain sloshing everywhere around him, Phil kept going toward the lake.

Mogi covered his mouth to keep from laughing. Phil was going to barge right into the Russian operation!

He focused on keeping his breath low and hiding from Phil when he heard a loud, sputtering sound—mechanical and sharp—coming from above him.

What in the world? It sounded like a chainsaw. Maybe the Russians had brought ground troops or something.

CHAPTER

As cautiously as he could, as quietly as he could, Mogi worked his way back to the trail, staying low to blend in with the blackness of the tree trunks. He was hoping he could watch the goings-on without being discovered.

Wow. They were really quiet. They weren't making any noise at all.

Mogi expected that a helicopter would be hovering above the water's surface as the plutonium cases were hooked onto cables. It shouldn't have taken divers very long to dig through the darkness of the muddy, ash-soaked water to find the plane, locate the cases, and get them connected to hoisting cables. In fact, they might lift the plane and drag it to the bank of the lake to make it easier.

He wasn't sure if they would have shot Phil first or waited until later, or maybe handcuffed him to a tree and given him a drug that made him forget everything he had witnessed. He was sure only that it was going to be a quick operation, in and out, deadly force if necessary, take no prisoners, leave no witnesses. He'd seen it done in plenty of movies.

Slowly creeping forward, watching intently, Mogi finally reached the lake. He saw the water through the fog, steam, and rain. Then he slowly stood and walked to the shoreline, his feet making noisy sucking sounds as he plunged through the sodden ash and mud.

Nothing. Nobody. No helicopter, no team of divers, no guns, no activity at all. Although the lake looked like a lumpy layer of coals, nothing disturbed its surface.

Nothing.

His shoulders slumped with the weight of the rain, and everything left his mind except for one familiar thought: Will I ever get tired of being a fool?

That's when Phil, covered with mud and ash, tackled him from behind.

"You're mine, you little creep! I'm going to show you how to have respect, one inch of flesh at a time!"

Their bodies landed in the mess of ash and water and mud and sticks and logs at the edge of the lake, with Phil on top. Mogi used his knees to throw him back. Phil came back swinging, but slipped in the mud as Mogi fell on top of him.

The two fighters were too busy to notice that the raucous, ratcheting sound had grown and now blared around them.

A dirt bike slid sideways off the trail and onto the shore, two black-helmeted riders covered in ash and dirt yelling at both of them.

Mogi had caught Phil with one good hit, but then found himself mired in mud and ash up to his knees. Phil was about to whack him a good one when the dirt bike slid in next to him, the driver's boot connecting hard enough to send Phil flying into the water.

"Mogi!" a voice was screaming, reaching for his hands and pulling his shirt. "Get on! Get on!"

He had no strength to resist. Good or bad, he grabbed the hand and launched himself out of the mud and onto the back of the bike. He only had room to sit down because the second rider had stood up. He grabbed onto those legs and held tight.

The dirt bike driver gunned the motor and took off in a wallow, slipping, sliding, and forcing the bike through the muck, almost losing both passengers.

The front wheel pulled off the ground as the driver struggled to keep the bike upright and going forward. Spraying ash, dirt, rocks, charcoal, and water, the back wheel found traction, and Mogi held tight as they climbed the trail that he had cartwheeled down only two days before.

High enough on the trail to escape the danger, the bike pulled over and stopped. Its passengers looked back and saw a wall of semi-solid water about eight feet high gush from the upper part of the canyon and hit the lake's surface with a slap, sending a tremendous wave across the lake. Following the initial wall, an ooze of mud, ash, trees, and logs flowed into the lake, so much that it seemed half of the lake was filled.

"Look!" Mogi pointed to the middle of the lake.

The wall of water and mud had pushed under the lake's surface, shoving the years-old bottom forward into a big mound. A piece of metal emerged from the soup of ash and burnt logs.

Over a few seconds, the tail of an airplane slowly rose out of the water.

The riders raised their visors and stared as the tail continued to rise. Just before it was straight in the air, it groaned to a halt.

Mogi looked into the faces that were now looking at him: Jennifer, covered with sweat and ash, and a driver with a big grin.

Muck Jones!

"Is that what I think it is?" Muck asked. "Is that Nancy's plane? It's been here all these years?"

"Yeah," Mogi said. "That's her plane."

Mogi was too exhausted to say anything more. He looked at his rescuers. "Uh. . .thanks."

Muck leaned his head back and gave a long laugh. "You need to thank your sister. When she couldn't keep you from going, she had the good sense to get me on the radio."

He pointed at the lake. "Take a look at that."

Clinging onto the side of the plane, Phil Agnew had survived the torrent of water coming down the canyon.

"You know," Muck said, looking at his passengers. "I didn't see my life as being so dull until you Franklins came along!"

CHAPTER

Six months later

Jim Daniels reached out and shook Mogi's hand. "Good to see you again."

Mogi smiled. It was going to be a great night. Nancy was there, and Muck, and he'd seen Dr. Soboknov across the room. And, of course, there was Jennifer and the rest of the two crews that made up the Fire Survivors.

It didn't seem like six months had gone by, but it had taken that long for the Los Alamos museum to get the exhibit ready. They had wanted to display the plane out in the parking lot, but the Smithsonian had claimed it for restoration.

Even without it, Mogi thought the museum had done a fine job.

The espionage exhibit now stood in the center of the entry hall. Each section had been redone, and a new display case had been added to hold the original airport log, Mogi's copy of the decoded message, a model of one of the recovered containment cases, the wheel found by Mogi and Charlotte, and other artifacts.

To the side of the display case was an enlargement of Nancy attending a White House ceremony where the president had signed a special congressional declaration that replaced Chris Johnson and Henry Sample's treason convictions with presidential medals, the highest peacetime honor granted by the federal government.

It had taken almost two weeks to pull the plane out of Guaje Lake and transport it to the Los Alamos airport, where it was taken apart and shipped to the Smithsonian. The cases of plutonium, of course, were taken out before the plane was moved, as well as the skeletal remains of the pilot and co-pilot; the mud had done a surprisingly good job of preserving them. Only five of the six cases were found, though, which prompted the researching of Russian intelligence files for the whole story.

There *was* a third man. It was known during the trial but never revealed because of the sensitivity of the organization to which he belonged. His organization swore that in no way could he have been connected with the attempted theft and demanded that he be treated as a non-issue. As it turned out, that non-issue was a long-planted Soviet operative who had worked undercover for a decade.

The Soviet hijacking plan had been to transfer the cases into different vehicles driven in different directions; if one were captured, the others still had considerable amounts of the nuclear fuel. The plane would be left at the field.

But something went wrong, and the plane took off immediately after touching down. The Soviet agent inside the plane had been shot, but had grabbed one of the cases and jumped through the cabin door. The people on the ground attempted to shoot the plane down, but it disappeared into the darkness.

With everything bungled, the single case and the agent's body were recovered, all pieces of the plane cut off by the barbed wire fence were hidden in one of the vehicles, and the operation vanished into the emptiness that is New Mexico. They had left only the airfield lanterns.

The Soviets waited for news of the botched robbery, but none came. After a few years of no information, the picture of the plutonium cases in the warehouse was created and leaked to stir the pot a little. With no reaction, it was assumed that the United States had not recovered the plane, and further inquiries were terminated.

It was a mystery for everybody and, having narrowly avoided being caught, the Soviets ceased to pursue the matter.

Professor Soboknov, of course, was not a spy. Not only was he not a spy, but it was through his contacts that the Soviet side of the operation was revealed. He was a very nice man, as Mogi had thought in the first place. Nancy and the professor worked hard to piece together the whole story and worked with the museum to construct the exhibit. A book deal was already being worked out.

As the opening of the exhibit began, the director of the laboratory stood and spoke: "It is the highest compliment to parents when they see their children function well in a situation that has never been imagined, and for which they have not been prepared. Will the parents of these children please stand and be recognized." The crowd erupted in thunderous applause.

"And then I would also like to ask Doctor Nancy Simpson to come forward and be with our young heroes." The Fire Survivors crowded onto the stage. Nancy smiled brightly as she moved next to them.

"It is with great honor," the director said, "that I am in the presence of these people. There is no greater symbol of a free America than that of a teacher surrounded by her students. It was their resourcefulness, their courage, and their coming together when threatened by an unimaginable situation that brings them tonight's recognition. But that coming together, that willingness to care and value each other, was no accident. It is because of the efforts of teachers such as Nancy, that we can count on a continuing legacy of young people who will make us all proud."

There were other words, but Mogi had stopped listening. He suddenly remembered the moment when everyone was crowding in next to him at the lake and wondering what to do. He had heard the roar—that deafening, hold-your-ears roar—of the fire dragon as it began its assault on the canyon. He remembered the ache as all hope left him.

He looked at the teen-agers around him on the stage. He would have never made it without them, and they would never have made it without him.

"Thank you," Nancy said as the applause quieted. She moved to the microphone.

"I have always been hopeful in my life that there is something inside of us that can only be satisfied by the relationships we make with each other and the bonds we create with the earth around us. I have been so lucky, so unbelievably lucky, to be able to work with young people in the setting that I do, and with the others who help me."

She smiled almost shyly at Muck.

"But tonight, if I may, I want to remember my father as well. I have waited many years for his true story to be told, and it would have remained lost forever if it hadn't been for one special student."

Nancy asked Mogi to step forward. He felt his legs shaking and knew he was glowing with embarrassment. She took a small object from her pocket.

"There has come into my life an angel. He worked with his friends to deliver all of them from death, and he worked to deliver my father back to me. I would like my angel to have his wings."

She opened her hand to reveal a small pin, a small flyer's insignia—two silver wings surrounding a red "A" for aviator.

Mogi watched as she gingerly pinned the wings above his pocket, surrounded by the wet spots made by the tears falling from his cheeks.

COMING IN SPRING 2018
Book 6 of the Mogi Franklin Mysteries: The Lady in White

Hundreds of cattle are mysteriously dying on one of the largest ranches in New Mexico. Mogi Franklin, working there as a cowboy over the summer vacation, finds himself embroiled in the life of a boy who was kidnapped by the Comanche Indians in 1871. In *The Lady in White,* the sixth book of the exciting Mogi Franklin Mysteries, he comes face-to-face with the ghost of the boy's mother, and must face the reality of the past to save the ranch from the enemies of the present.

ABOUT THE AUTHOR

Don Willerton was raised in a small oil boomtown in the Panhandle of Texas, becoming familiar through family vacations with the northern New Mexico area where he now makes his home.

After earning a degree in physics from Midwestern State University in Texas and a master's in computer science and electrical engineering from the University of New Mexico, he worked for Los Alamos National Laboratory for almost three decades.

During his career there, Willerton was a supercomputer programmer for a number of years and a manager after that for "way too long," and also worked on information policy and cyber-security.

He finds focusing on only one thing very difficult among such varied interests as home building, climbing Colorado's tallest peaks, and rafting the rivers of the Southwest (including the Colorado through Grand Canyon). Willerton also has owned a handyman business for a number of years, rebuilt old cars, and made furniture in his woodshop.

He is a wanderer in both mind and body, fascinated with history and its landscape, varied peoples and their cultures, good mysteries, secrets, and seeking out treasure. Most of all, he loves the outdoors and the places he finds in the Southwest where spirits live and ghosts dance. Weaving it all together to share with readers has been the driving force of Willerton's writing over the past twenty years.

The Lake of Fire is the fifth novel in the nine-book Mogi Franklin series of Southwest-based mysteries for middle-grade boys and girls.